Enough

Nicole Baker

Edited by: Jen Suever

Contents

Prologue

Jameson

Sixteen Years Ago

Winter is my favorite time of the year. The cold numbs my limbs, which goes well with the numbness of my heart. I learned a long time ago to turn off my emotions. Life was easier that way. As I walk through the streets of Chicago, I take in the dirty streets filled with garbage, and I accept that this is my life now. There was a time it was filled with happiness and laughter. When winter days were filled with snowball fights in the backyard followed by hot cocoa by the fireplace. Those days are gone, the sting of the wind equates to the sting I feel when I think of those memories. I wish I didn't remember. Sometimes I think if I had no memories of the life I once had, I wouldn't feel so bitter about what I lost.

Yesterday was my thirteenth birthday. It came and went without anybody remembering. Maybe they did remember, they just didn't care. Truth is, I wasn't expecting to be acknowledged. It's safer not to expect anything out of life anymore.

When I make it to end of the street, I take a deep breath before I make my way inside the place that I now call home. Laura, my foster mother, is in the kitchen cooking dinner. She may be the only good thing about living here. She isn't particularly nice, but she is not cruel. She gives me space when I need it and cooks me breakfast, lunch, and dinner. Sometimes I wonder what she sees in Frank. When he isn't watching sports wasted on the couch, he is in her face about something. He is angry at the world and seems to take it out on everyone else around him, myself included.

I hang my backpack and heavy winter coat on the row of hooks provided for us foster kids. Laura likes to keep things clean. I try to make sure the salt and water from my boots do not get all over the hardwood floor.

There are four of us that are living here right now, all sharing a room with two bunk beds. It can be hard to never have any space to yourself, but the guys aren't so bad. Things could be worse. Alan once told me that one of the guys in his old foster house used to bully everyone. He would make them hand over any money they earned shoveling snow or mowing lawns. Since I'm an only child, living with other kids is new to me. It's been a couple years, but it's still hard to get used to.

I walk on the old wooden floor, around the corner to the family room where Frank is watching football with a drink in his hand. I try to creep away without being seen.

"Where do you think you're going?" Frank croaks.

"Upstairs," I answer.

Fewer words are best with him. You never know how drunk he is or what mood he's in.

"Whatever, little shit."

I'm not sure if he knows I can hear it when he mumbles those words. They used to sting, now they just flow right through me. I don't need to be liked by Frank, just to be left alone.

Slowly, I take the stairs one at a time, trying not to make too much noise. Habit of trying to be invisible wherever I go. Once I make it to my room, I notice the two bunkbeds in each corner are empty. No one else is home. This is one of the only times I feel like I can truly relax. I lay down on my bottom bunk, grab my dirty dark blue comforter, and wrap myself up. I close my eyes and see my mom, laughing as we mix brownie batter together. We would always make a treat together after school, memories that I hold onto. They are the calm I need in order to fall asleep. I pretend it's real and that they never died. That the drunk driver never took them away from me.

I must have dozed off because I hear Frank screaming my name at the bottom of the stairs. Whipping the comforter off my body, I try to wake myself up enough to climb out of bed.

"Get down here you selfish bastard. How many times do I have to shout that dinner is ready?"

I stand up and run down the stairs in an effort to calm his temper before he gets really angry.

"Sorry, sir," I say before I take a seat next to Brad.

Everyone begins to dig in while the room is filled with a deafening silence. I'm not sure why Laura insists that we all eat together. It's clear that no one has any interest in being around each other. Frank seems to have tipped the scales from drunk to plastered. He can barely sit up straight in his chair.

I look down at the lasagna and want nothing more than to slowly eat and enjoy the dinner. Instead, I quickly inhale my food, not giving myself time to taste it. I would rather be upstairs in my room. The other guys tend to feel the same way I do. When I look around the table, they have their heads down as they quickly chew their food.

When I'm finished, I take my plate and walk over to the sink to rinse it and put it in the dishwasher. As I turn around, Frank is standing there with a grimace on his face.

"I didn't hear a thank you for dinner," he grumbles.

"Thanks," I say with my head down and try to walk around him.

He grabs me by the shirt collar and leans in, within inches of my face. I smell the mixture of beer and bourbon on his breath.

"That didn't sound like you meant it. You've some nerve treating me like that in my own home. One that I provide for you."

I try to take a step back to get some distance. He releases my collar and lets me go.

"I wish you wouldn't let me stay here," I mumble as I walk away.

I will later come back to this moment, where I could have walked away with my mouth shut. Why did I say something? Why did I have to open my damn mouth?

"What the hell did you just say?" he fires back.

I keep walking towards the stairs, knowing I just hit a nerve. Frank doesn't seem to think this conversation is over. I hear his footsteps as they approach from behind and I try to pick up the pace, only a couple of feet from the stairs. He's too quick, and I feel his calloused hand grab my neck and slam me to the ground. He crouches down and grabs my collar with one hand as I see his other hand make a fist. My eyes grow wide as they realize what he is about to do.

When his fist makes contact with my face, the pain is instant. I have never been punched before.

"You gonna get up and stand up for yourself, punk?" he spits at me. "Pay close attention boys. This is what happens when you disrespect me in my house."

He stands up until he is towering over me while I stair up at him, noticing the smug look in his eyes. They tell me that whatever he is about to do, he is going to enjoy it. Over the next couple minutes, he proceeds to kick me repeatedly until I finally hear a rib snap and scream out in agony. I think I can make out Laura in the background screaming for him to stop. He gives me one last kick for good measure, until I hear his footsteps retreating up the stairs. I try to sit up but the pain in my side is too intense. After what feels like forever, Jacob comes over.

"Dude, can you get up?"

I groan in response, shaking my head. "No," I barely get out.

"Fuck, what are we supposed to do?"

"I think we need to call 911." I hear Alan say in the background.

Eventually, the pain is so great that I pass out.

I wake up to bright lights and loud noises surrounding me. When I open my eyes, I see a nurse standing at the foot of a hospital bed. It takes me a minute to figure out why I'm here, until the pain brings me back to the memory of Frank kicking me. The nurse looks at me with unmistakable sympathy in her eyes.

"Are you feeling okay, honey?" Her voice is soft and soothing. I wish I could ask her to just keep talking to me, help ease some of this pain.

I shake my head up and down. What else am I supposed to say? I am alive, aren't I? That's the most okay I have been in years. Ever since the accident, where I lost everything.

"Now that you are awake, let me get you some more medicine for the pain."

After she gives me more medicine that takes the edge off, a police officer and social worker walk into my room.

"Good evening, Jameson," the officer says. "This is Ashley, your social worker. We are here to ask you a couple of questions."

I spend the next twenty minutes answering their endless list of questions. They told me that Frank is in jail and will likely be for a long time. The other guys in his foster care told them everything they saw. He is being charged for assault, among other things. You would think I would be relieved, but my soul just feels empty. He's behind bars, but I still have nothing.

"We are going to make sure you are taken care of. We have an incredible foster family lined up for you," Ashley tells me.

I nod my head in response. That's what they told me about Frank and Laura.

Chapter One

Peyton

"Peyton, can I see you in my office?" Lance, the vice president of my department asks me.

He's been my boss for three years now, since I was made Director of IT. We work for a top marketing agency in downtown Chicago. It's a great job with great benefits. It can be a bit stressful at times with a fair amount of overtime that can take away from my social life, but it's better than being broke. I stand up from my desk and leave my office, turning left to head into Lance's corner office right next door. I walk in and take a seat across from his desk.

"Peyton," he begins. He is in his sixties with gray beginning to take over his head of hair. "As you know, the board and management have been discussing investing in a new ERP system. Ours is twenty years old and extremely outdated. We need something that's going to help us keep up with our clients demands."

"Yes, sir. I agree. Our system just creates more work and manpower."

"Yes, exactly. I'm also only a year away from retirement. It doesn't make sense to make me be the source of all information regarding this massive undertaking. By the time we have selected a system and implemented it, I will be on my way out the door. Which is exactly why Jameson and I agreed that it made more sense if you took over this project. I don't need to tell you what kind of opportunity this is. Jameson himself wants to be closely involved in the process, which means you will have one on one time to impress the CEO before I retire. He *will* be selecting my replacement."

"This is a huge opportunity sir. Thank you so much for trusting me to take it over."

"Non-sense, Peyton. You're the only one I trust to take this on in our department. Jameson would like to get a move on this as soon as possible. I told him I would talk to you this morning. He wants to schedule a meeting this afternoon for the three of us to go over strategy."

"Absolutely! I don't have any meetings scheduled for this afternoon. Anytime works for me."

"Very well. I will come around and grab you when it's time for the meeting. Congratulations, Peyton."

"Thank you, Lance!" I say as I stand up and shake his hand.

I try to make it back to my office before I let the huge grin take over my face. I can't believe they picked me to head this up. This is such a huge opportunity for someone in my field to take over. An ERP system is the backbone to any company. It effects all departments across the board, and the chance to work closely with the CEO is huge. I've never really gotten a chance to get to know him, he is very closed off. We have only ever spoken a few words to each other here and there around the office. Lance is always the one meeting with him. His good looks only add to the intimidation factor. He is tall and lean with the perfect amount of muscle. His strong jaw and blue eyes make his face hard to even look at without your heartrate increasing.

But I won't let that distract me from impressing him with my knowledge and dedication. This is about my career and the long hours finally paying off. The chance to snatch a VP position in my thirties, which would be impressive. I get an email notification that a meeting has been set for two-thirty with Jameson and Lance.

As soon as I get back to my office, I pick up the phone and call my friend Janet, who also works downtown. She is a paralegal for one of the top law firms in the city and has been my wingman ever since Blake went off and got married. Even though Blake is divorced now, she is the more low-key kind of friend. The one you call to watch reruns of Friends while you eat cheesecake directly out of the box. Don't get me wrong, you need both kinds of friends in your life. There are sometimes the last thing I want to do is get dressed up and worry about fending off creeps all night.

"Hello?" Janet answers.

"What are you doing for lunch today?" I ask in a hurry.

"Ummm, I haven't even thought about it yet. Are you okay?" she questions.

"Yes! I just got offered the chance to work with the CEO and head up the development of a *new* ERP system!"

"Peyton, that's sounds amazing! Good for you!" Janet says enthusiastically.

I can always count on her to match my tone of excitement. I swear, sometimes, I could care less whether she means it or not. I just appreciate the gesture.

"Thanks! It's such an amazing opportunity *and* I'm meeting with the CEO after lunch today."

"Aahh, and you need some of my expert confidence boosting speeches?"

"Yes! Please, tell me you're free."

"You're in luck; I'm not meeting with any clients today. Where and when?"

"Giovanni's at noon," I confirm.

Thankfully, it's already eleven-thirty so I head to the restroom to freshen up. When I'm finished, I decide to head out now to make sure I can get us a table. Going to lunch at noon in the city is chaos. When I walk into the restaurant, the owner spots me.

"Ah, Miss Peyton, so nice to see you!" he comes over and gives me a kiss on each cheek. Roberto is in his sixties and as Italian as they come.

"Roberto, my favorite person!" I reply.

"Come sei dolce. You are too kind! Come, I give you my best table."

He seats me in the table off in the corner, away from the commotion. I text Janet to let her know where I am and order us our meals. We skip the slow chatter while perusing the menu before deciding on a dish that is going to take forever. No one has time for that. Whoever gets their first, orders the food!

"Ugh, I finally made it. I hope you weren't waiting too long." Janet startles me from the email I was just sending out.

I wave her off like it's no big deal. "Come on, no need to worry about that. I called you last minute. I'm just thankful you could make it!"

"Of course. So, what're we eating today?" she asks over her glass of sparkling water.

"Italian braised beef ragu with parmesan polenta."

"Oh, hell yes!"

I laugh. "I know, it sounds amazing! I'm going to need to hit the gym tonight to work it off, but it's worth it!"

"So, tell me about this project," Janet asks.

I go into detail about what it takes to get a system like this up and running. She takes the time to listen to what I say, asking questions when she doesn't quite understand something. Some people think because she is gorgeous and outgoing that she must not be smart, but she is a killer combination.

"So, you need to impress this CEO if he will be the one interviewing your boss's replacement," she says as our food is being served.

"Yes, exactly!"

"How well do you know him?"

"I don't know him at all. We have offered a hello to each other on the *rare* occasion we're in the elevator together."

We both stop talking while we moan over our first bites of our lunch because well...food!

"Oh my god, I never want to stop eating this!" I say with a mouthful.

"Not if I beat you to it," Janet replies.

It takes us a minute or two to regroup and remember what we were talking about before our food orgasms began.

"Anyway, what were we talking about? Oh, you basically have never had a full conversation with the boss."

"Yeah, and he seems super intimidating! Not to mention he is insanely good looking."

"Come on! Peyton...intimidated?" she looks at me with surprise written all over her face.

It's true, I'm rarely intimidated by much. I'm usually the life of the party, the one willing to take a risk. I'm not quite sure what it is about him that makes me feel so uptight.

"I know, it's crazy...*I'm* being crazy."

"Nah, good looks and power will do that to any woman. Just fake it, doesn't matter if you're feeling confidant on the inside, just make sure he thinks you feel it!"

"Fake it... well I've done that plenty of times before with good looking men," I wiggle my eyebrows.

"Ugh, haven't we all." Janet rolls her eyes.

After we pay for lunch and part ways, I'm feeling much better about this meeting. I may not feel as confident as I would like, but like Janet said, no one needs to know that.

I get back to my desk and look through my emails, trying to filter through all the junk that I get copied on. Sometimes I just want to write back and yell I DO NOT NEED TO KNOW ANY OF THIS to everyone. If it doesn't pertain to me or anything my staff and I work on, please leave me off the email for the love of God!

"You ready?" Lance startles me at my door.

I look at my computer screen, surprised to see it is two-twenty already. I grab my laptop and follow Lance to the elevators. We work on the fifty-eighth floor; the CEO's office is on the seventy-fifth floor. I've never been up there. I can't help but fidget as I watch the numbers climb on the elevator until it dings, signaling our arrival. We walk out of the elevator and head straight to the reception desk. The woman, who I know as Angela, offers a smile when she sees us walking up.

"Hello, Lance. Hello, Peyton. How are you two this afternoon?"

"Fine, thank you," Lance replies. I offer a smile and nod.

"Mr. Davis is ready for you."

She points us in what must be the direction of his office. We begin walking down the hallway to the left of Angela's desk, until we reach the end where Jameson's door is located. Lance knocks on the door with the confidence that I wish I had at the moment.

"Come in," a deep and commanding voice announces. I wipe my hands on my skirt, hoping to get rid of any moisture.

I'm normally more confident in these types of situations. I don't know what is making my nerves feel so out of control.

It could be that I have never worked closely with such a powerful and intimidating man before. I don't want to screw up this opportunity by overstepping my boundaries with my opinions that I can feel quite strongly about.

Lance opens the door and walks in first. He leads us over to Jameson's desk at the far end of the room. Jameson looks deep in thought as he looks at his computer. He pays no attention to us as we make our way in and stand in front of the chairs opposite him. Lance must know not to interrupt him, because he stands there in silence. Apparently, this is a do-not-speak-unless-spoken-to situation.

I use this opportunity to take in his office. It has a minimalist kind of vibe going on. He has a long dark wood desk that stretches half the length of the room with only his computer and keyboard on the top. The chairs are all cream colored and are big and inviting. Behind me to my right are four more of the large cream chairs surrounded a circular brown coffee table. On the other side is a long white marble conference table with eight conference chairs surrounding it. There are a couple plants strategically placed around the office, but no personal touches like certificates or picture frames.

After several minutes of us patiently waiting for him to acknowledge our presence, he finally looks up at us while he stands. I'm struck by his eyes as they look me up and down before moving back over to Lance.

"Lance," he says as he shakes his hand. His mesmerizing eyes glance back in my direction as he offers me his hand. "Ms. Brady, nice to officially meet you." I guess the other times we met were not "official" in his brain. *Good to know!*

"Nice to meet you as well, Mr. Davis." I obviously didn't say that last thought to him.

"James will do."

"James, you can call me Peyton."

He nods before he gestures for us to take a seat.

"Peyton, I trust that Lance has filled you in on what we are looking for in our new system."

"Yes, he has. I have some prior experience being a part of the process for selecting a new ERP system. I wasn't part of the decision making but was there to lend a helping hand along the way which gave me some great experience."

"Well, I'm sure what we are looking for is quite different. I'll need you to be on top of your game. The company is willing to invest a very generous amount of money to get the right system with the right team to implement it. I expect nothing but the best from you."

So, it sounds like he is going to be a dick about it. I hate when people talk to me like I am a child and that I wouldn't give my best unless told otherwise. He can get off his high horse and realize that we are all adults and don't need to be spoken to like that.

"I assure you that this project will have my full time and attention. I understand the enormity of the task," I reply, hoping that is enough to sooth his ego.

"Good, we need to begin as soon as possible. I would like to be meeting with vendors by the end of the month. That gives us three weeks to dive in and figure out exactly what we're looking for."

"Three weeks? That seems a little rushed. I think it would be beneficial if we take a little bit more time to analyze our current processes to know exactly what we need to improve. The presentations these vendors give can take days and are very tedious at times. We need to have a good understanding of what we're looking for."

"Are you suggesting that I don't know my companies processes well enough to be ready in three weeks?"

Is he serious right now? Yes, that is exactly what I'm suggesting. No one knows that amount of information from a company of this size. We're talking about knowing exactly what all one hundred and fifty corporate employees do on a day-to-day basis. No one knows that without meeting with management and gaining some insight. I go to say these very words when Lance beats me to the punch.

"We understand that you know exactly what you're looking for. Peyton will be here to offer whatever advice that she can along the way. She is a very bright woman. I'm sure she will be a great asset to you."

"Yes, we will have to see about that," James replies, and I'm close to standing up and walking out of this office right now. Have I done something to offend him?

"Three weeks is doable, but we need to get started right away."

"Which is what I have already suggested."

What a dick!

"Lance, thank you for bringing Peyton to my office. You can get back to work while her and I get further acquainted."

"Yes, you two have a lot to discuss." Lance stands up and begins to walk towards the door. I want to scream for him to take me with him, do not leave me alone in this room with this devil of a man. For the benefit of my career, I keep my mouth shut and try to find the courage to continue this meeting.

"First things first, let's get a schedule together over the next couple weeks of when we will meet," Lance leans back in his chair.

I try not to sneak a peak in the direction of his stomach and waist that are now on display for me as he puts his hands behind his head. Keep eye contact, Peyton. Do not get caught looking in the direction anywhere *near* your bosses' private parts. It does not matter how good looking he is, his personality kills all of it.

"Do you have a schedule in mind?" I ask.

"I was thinking we should meet for at least a couple hours every day, at least in the beginning. The rest of the time will likely be spent researching vendors or gathering data from our departments."

While all of this sounds amazing, I can't help but wonder how I will have time to fulfill my other obligations. I'm in the middle of organizing a complete overhaul of one of our payroll systems. It will definitely affect the team if I just bow out right now.

"That schedule works for me. I'll of course need some time each day to dedicate to my current duties."

James sits up straight folding his hands over his desk. "I thought Lance already spoke to you about the expectations. If you were to come on board with this project, I need your full time and attention on this tight of a deadline. You'll need to delegate your current duties to your staff."

No, Lance did not discuss that with me. I don't like the idea of handing off this project without some sort of advanced notice to get my team up to speed. Rachel is an excellent team member, but there is no way she's going to take this payroll project on without hiccups along the way. Typical CEO, just thinking everyone needs to drop whatever they are doing on a whim to cater to his demands.

"I'm sorry, sir. I wasn't informed of that, but I'm not sure it is in the best interest of the company for me to drop my current project. This payroll upgrade is extremely important to execute flawlessly. You can imagine what would happen if everyone's paychecks weren't correct or not issued on time."

He dramatically looks up at the ceiling, as if my concern is annoying him. God forbid he care about his employee's well-being.

"I trust that you and Lance have hired a competent staff. Unless you think we should take a look at whether or not some of them still deserve a spot at this company."

I narrow my eyes at him, in complete disgust at the audacity he has to insult our team. Everyone works their ass off for this company.

"No," I bite out. "They're excellent employees."

"Well then, they should have no problem taking over your duties. Moving on, I would like to put it on our calendar to have hired a vendor three weeks from today."

This deadline is completely unrealistic. We are going to be working here until midnight every night if he wants us to be prepared enough to make a decision in three weeks. Each vendor offers very different benefits and has a certain number of drawbacks. You have to figure out which features are the most important and what you are willing to compromise to get there.

"About the deadline. Are you sure three weeks is enough time? I have been on a project like this before and it took the team six months to feel comfortable making the final call on the software. This software is what the company will have to live with for the next thirty years."

If looks could kill, Mr. Davis would have murdered me with his eyes just now. He clearly is not used to any kind of pushback.

"The timeline is three weeks. I don't know what kind of indecisive people you worked with prior to this company, but I'm confident that I can make a decision that is good for the company on that timeline. Now, do you have any other objections before we continue?"

Yes, as a matter of fact I do! I object to working with such an egotistical jackass. One who is stupidly handsome which is probably the only reason he could get a woman to voluntarily spend their time with him.

"No, I don't. Please, go on."

"Now, I would like to start tomorrow at 8 AM sharp. Our first order of business will be to start looking over the finance departments major pain points. I've already requested a list of responsibilities from each team member for us to get a rough idea. Does that work for you, Peyton?"

His last question is asked in a mocking tone. I can tell he expects me to give my two cents on where we should start. Lucky for him, I completely agree that we need to start with the finance department.

I nod my head up and down, frustrated that I have nothing to come back at him with. He looks at me and I swear I catch a small smirk on his lips. It's so subtle that I could be mistaken.

"Okay, well, that is all for today. I look forward to working with you."

He stands up and offers me his hand. This time when I place my hand in his, the warmth and strength behind his shake sends shivers up my spine. I refuse to acknowledge my reaction.

"Thank you. I look forward to working with you too, sir."

Maybe if I say that to myself enough times, it will become true. But right now, I don't look forward to being in this man's presence every single day for the next three weeks.

Chapter Two

James

I don't know why I acted like that. Normally, someone questioning me or offering their perspective is welcomed. The second she began to question my judgement, my ego took a hit. It doesn't help that she's breathtakingly beautiful. Her curves were taunting me in her skirt which hugs her ass and leads up to a petite waist. She has light brown hair with streaks of caramel in it that highlight her green eyes. I've seen her around the office, and we have exchanged a few words, but I always hold out because my attraction to her is inappropriate. I always seem to picture her in compromising positions with less clothing on, not something that's appropriate for your Director of IT.

Luckily, it's already five o'clock, giving me a good cut off so I can escape work on time for once and hit the gym. As I'm walking out, I see Angela packing up her stuff. She never leaves until I do or until I dismiss her. She's a great assistant and the only one I have ever had that was not afraid to stand up to me. It doesn't hurt that she is sixty and been through enough crap in her lifetime to refuse to put up with mine.

"I'll see you tomorrow morning, Angela," I say as I pass by her desk. She looks up at me with wide eyes.

"Leaving so soon? It's only five."

"Yes, I think I have had enough for today."

Meaning I've had enough of a certain employee taking up too much of my brain space. I can tell Peyton is going to be a feisty one who will fight with me tooth and nail until she gets her way.

"Very well. See you tomorrow, boss."

Once I'm out the door and into the warm summer breeze, I loosen my tie and walk the two blocks to my gym. I head to the locker room where I can change into my gray shorts and dark blue t-shirt. First, I decide to hit the weights. Todays my day for high rep, low weight but I don't have the patience for that. I decide I need to blow off as much steam as possible and go for the high weight, low reps. I'm by no means a built guy compared to some of the other guys that work out here, but I have a good six pack with some nice arm definition to get with it. The ladies certainly like what they see. I'm taking a breath, sweat pouring down my face as a blonde beauty walks by and checks out my backside, not so subtly.

After spending about thirty minutes lifting weights and doing crunches, which is my normal routine, I decide I still need to exert more energy. Some time on the treadmill should help with that. I rarely make my way over to this side of the gym, preferring to get my run in outside on different days. When I approach the long line of treadmills facing the windows, I spot an empty one at the end of the row next to a brunette. I try not to look at her ass in those yoga pants, but my eyes have a mind of their own and sometimes I just can't control them.

I step on to the treadmill and start off at a fast-walking pace to get my body ready. I look over at the brunette's screen next to me and see that she's jogging at six miles per hour. Next thing I know, she kicks it up to an eight. Did she see me look at her screen and want to prove something to me? I decide to get straight into my run and begin to go at an eight as well. I can feel her eyeing me and I smirk. I haven't seen her face yet and

I still hesitate to get caught looking so I keep my eyes facing forward. The feisty woman hits the up arrow until she is now running at a nine.

I chuckle at her tenacity. I'm a good eight inches taller than her; she cannot outrun me. I decide to end the game right away when I hit twelve and begin sprinting. Hearing an audible grunt of frustration come from my left, I decide to steal a glance at my competitor. See who wanted to show me up so badly. When I look to my left and see Peyton glaring at me, I almost lose my balance and bite it. Luckily, I catch myself and lower my speed to a jog so get back in control.

"Mr. Davis! Are you alright?" Peyton looks over at me with a concerned face.

"I'm fine," I bark out.

She seems to note the anger in my response and matches my look with her own of frustration. She turns her head back to the windows and continues her jog. After about twenty minutes, she slows herself down to a walk and grabs her water bottle. I can't help but gaze at her delicate neck as I watch her guzzle her drink. She's very petite for a woman who puts out so much energy in the room.

After a couple more minutes, I decide to cool down as I click the number three on the screen. I'm panting and sweating but feel as good as I always do after a run. It doesn't take me long to regain control of my heartrate, a sign of good cardiovascular health I'm told. I try to watch what I put in my mouth and maintain a workout routine.

"Glad you caught yourself before you stumbled off that machine. That would've hurt, going the speed that you were."

Peyton smiles at me with humor in her eyes.

"Yeah, it happens when you can run that fast. Not that you would know what it's like."

She *laughs* at my insult, and I can't help but roll my eyes at her.

"I look forward to working together, *Mr. Davis*," she barks out at me before hopping off her machine and heading towards the locker room.

Why is she so infuriating? Not only is she beautiful, but she can hold her own. It's a killer combination. One that I'm not used to coming across. Most women want me for my money and looks. She seems to want nothing to do with me and is not intimidated by my status in the company. Maybe this will actually be a bit of fun, I smirk to myself as I walk into the locker room.

"Morning, Angela," I say as I walk past her desk towards my office.

"Morning, boss!" she says without looking up from her computer.

That's one thing I love about her; she isn't into small talk or bullshit. We speak when business requires to do so. I glance at my watch and realize it's already seven-fifty. I meant to get in earlier to prepare for my meeting with Peyton this morning, but I had such a hard time falling asleep, that I slept through my alarm. I'm slightly rattled and unprepared for the day, a feeling I loathe. I only have time to get my computer started and look through a couple emails before Peyton is at my door.

"Hello, Mr. Davis," Peyton speaks as she walks towards my desk.

"*Peyton*, good morning. I thought we already established that we would greet each other on a first name basis."

"You're right. I'm sorry. Good morning, *James.*"

"Let's take a seat over here at the conference table."

I usher her to the table set up on one side of my office with a tv and projector hanging on the wall.

We take a seat and stare at each other, both waiting for the other to speak first. It feels like we are fighting for the upper hand in this working relationship. My eyes graze her body as I notice what she is wearing. She has on a black pant suit with a white dress shirt underneath that cuts just above her cleavage. I'm tempted to lean forward to get a glance down her top. I almost visibly shake my head to get these thoughts to stop, it's thoughts like this that will make me weak. After several minutes of silence, I see her frustration beginning to build.

"Would you like me to start the meeting, sir?" she huffs out.

ma'am, I think I can handle it," I fire back. "I believe we were going to begin with the finance department. Let me put this report I have on the projector."

I feel her eyes on me as I work to get everything up and running. This is why I like to get to work early and be prepared. It makes me look weak if I don't have everything ready to go. This projector should have been on and waiting before she walked through my door. I will need to make sure Angela knows that all my meetings with Peyton will require the use of the projector and conference table. I hope my refrigerator is properly stocked with refreshments.

"Okay," I begin. "I have emailed this to you to go over at your leisure. What we have are tabs from each manager within the department, giving a list of all the tasks their employees positions have with a brief description of each task. I asked them to highlight any task that they believe is a major pain point of the department. I would like to begin with diving into some of the highlighted tasks to see exactly what the major issues are they are facing."

"Okay, what are you thinking? Would you like me to take accounts payable while you takes accounts receivable, and we can divvy up the rest as we complete them. We can take notes about what we find and brainstorm off each other as we go," she suggests.

"I think that works for now. We can adjust as we go if we feel it is not an efficient use of our time."

She nods her head in agreement and we both get to work reading through the notes. The first thing I realize, is that they have highlighted a lot. I understand that to them, all their tasks can feel like they are not being done efficiently, but without giving me a good starting point of the *most* painful ones, it creates more reading for me in the beginning.

After what feels like the entire afternoon, but was only an hour, I drop my pen and lean back in my chair. Peyton glances over at me as I rub my eyes which feel strained from the screen.

"What have you found so far?" she asks.

I lean back up in my chair and grab my notepad. "Well, first thing I realized is that they seem to think anything that requires actual work from them is a major pain point. I feel like every task was highlighted."

She cracks a smile at me. "I think my manager felt the same way. She even highlighted their process of cutting checks which, I'm sorry, is always labor intensive."

"Next thing I noticed is that our process for collecting our debts is way too labor intensive and the reports they need to manually generate eat up way too much time. If we could get more real time data on our collections, we could be collecting much more cash and improve our cash flow."

"Ok, that'is a good one to look out for in our search for the right system."

We spend the rest of the afternoon going through all of the information and making a list of the top processes that we would like to see improved in the new software. When it reaches noon, the end of our scheduled meeting, I close my laptop.

"Well, looks like it's lunch time already. I'm almost done anyways. I'll wrap up my notes after lunch," I tell her.

She begins to pack up her things, bending over the table to reach for some papers. I get the glimpse down her shirt I was hoping for this morning, and the view does not disappoint.

She has on a black lace bra that seems to push up her luscious breasts. I quickly try to divert my eyes before she catches me.

"Sounds good. I'm basically done. Are we going to meet same time tomorrow?"

"Actually, I have an important meeting with the board in the morning, so we will need to make the meeting in the afternoon. I'll have Angela set up a meeting invite."

She nods her head. "Works for me. I'll see you tomorrow, *boss*."

I narrow my eyes at her, sensing she said that with a sarcastic undertone. I don't know why we have this push and pull between us. Either way, we will have to figure out how to work with each other.

I spent the entire evening last night pulling together the top eight systems that I would like to review. Each of them have an introductory video to watch ranging from twenty to forty-five minutes long. After the meeting I had this morning with the board, I'm feeling the pressure to get this project moving forward quickly so I have more updates to give.

We have to watch these videos this afternoon and gain some insight into what type of features are out there for us. We only have three hours scheduled today from two to five, but we have some other things to go over first. I hear a knock at my open door and look up to see Peyton standing there in a tight green dress with a slit up the right leg.

"Good afternoon, James," she says.

"Good afternoon, Peyton. How has your day been?"

She seems to take that as a sign to come in and walks in, heading towards the conference table to deposit her things.

"It's been crazy. I've been trying to get the staff ready to take over my current projects."

"I see. Well, if you need any help with getting those projects running smoothly, please let Lance know. There's no reason he shouldn't be able to offer his assistance."

She looks up at me like she is surprised I have a nice bone in my body.

"Thank you, I'll keep that in mind."

"So, where shall we start today?" she asks.

"I was thinking we can finish where we left off yesterday. Go over what we came up with from each manager. Get on the same page about our top priorities."

I meet her at the conference table, and we get comfortable as we take turns telling each other about our thoughts on some of the current processes our finance department is using. It takes a bit longer than I would have liked. Once we are wrapping up, the time is already four-thirty. I see her look down at her watch and hope she is not itching to get out of here. We're not going anywhere anytime soon. We have got to take a look at these videos and get some good notes on what kind of options are out there.

"I was hoping we were going to get that done faster," I begin. "I have ten introduction videos that we need to watch and take notes on. I'll tell Angela to go ahead and order dinner for us."

"Okay, I can work late tonight. Thank you for asking so nicely." I think I catch a slight eye roll.

I have enough stress with the board breathing down my throat. The last thing that I need is an employee giving me a hard time. I stand up from the table and put my hands down, leaning closer to her.

"Ms. Brady, this project is going to take some serious dedication. Now, if you're not up to the task, please tell me now so I can find someone who is."

She stands up and matches my posture on the other side of the table, leaving very little space between our faces.

"Mr. Davis, I have absolutely no problem with my dedication. I already told you I'm up for working late and putting in the extra hours. What I would like is some respect for my time and a simple question on whether tonight works for me. I don't appreciate demands or assumptions that I'm at your beck and call."

Her breaths are coming quickly, and I look down at her chest, catching a glimpse of her breasts rising and falling. When I look back up into her eyes, I see them change from anger to lust. We are standing there, inches apart, both aware of the electricity coursing between us. I watch her bite down on her bottom lip and can feel myself stiffen in my pants. I need to step away before we do something stupid.

I stand up and take a step away from the table, clearing my throat.

"Very well, I will make sure to be more respectful of your time," I state before I turn around and head for my desk to tell Angela that we need dinner for tonight.

Chapter Three

Peyton

Why do I do this to myself? I should be kissing his ass. Although, he could be a bit nicer when he needs something from me. He is clearly used to people jumping through hoops for him. I watch him walk across the room and can't help that my eyes wonder down to his bottom. Why does his ass have to look so nice in those pants? After he tells Angela to place a delivery order for dinner, he looks back in my direction.

"Do you want to break for ten or fifteen and meet back in my office?"

"Yes, that would be great."

I walk out of his office and head for the elevators towards my office to grab my purse so I can head home as soon as we are done.

The office is beginning to head home for the day, people are packing up their things and closing down. Pretty soon, it'll be a ghost town and I'll be working here alone with James. The thought of being alone with him sends shivers down my spine. I can't tell if they are nerves or excitement.

Ten minutes later, I'm walking back into his office. James is currently on the phone, but waves me in. I notice he took off his suit jacket and rolled up his sleeves. His watch catches my eye as it first, it's masculine and expensive. It doesn't take long to catch his forearms and the veins running through them. I hate that I notice every sexy feature on this man.

"You ready to get started?" James stares at me with interest.

I must have been lost in thought for a while because I don't recall him getting off the phone. My cheeks feel warm, embarrassed by being caught starring.

"Yep, let's do it. Where should I setup?"

He points towards the chairs across from the conference table with considerably more cushion and room to relax in.

"Let's sit over here. We can face these towards the projector but be more comfortable."

We get the chairs setup and facing the right direction before he props an end table in front of us to hold his laptop. I pull out my notebook and get comfortable as he gets the first video going. The first three videos were on the shorter side and gave us some great insight. My hand is aching from taking so many notes. The fourth company is a total bust and after almost thirty minutes. We both eventually give up on taking notes.

"I think we veto this one. They don't offer the reporting capabilities that we are looking for," he slams his pen down on his notebook.

"Yes!" My head drops back out of frustration. "I completely agree! This one is a total waste of our time!"

"Alright, let's move on to video number five." He glances down at his watch. "Food should be here in thirty minutes. We can eat after this one."

It's almost seven and the sun is beginning to dip behind the clouds. The light in the room is beginning to dim, which would usually make me sleepy if I wasn't already wired from the man sitting next to me. Sometime during the video, I can't help but pay attention to the smell of his cologne. Our chairs are close enough that I keep getting hints of it every few minutes. I don't know what it is about scent for me, but it just does something. Too bad it's attached to a total dickhead of a boss. I look over at him and I think it's the position he is sitting, with his foot resting on his knee, that makes me see the outline of his dick. I can't help but zoom in on it as I start to picture what it would be like to run my tongue up and down his shaft.

I hear him clear his throat and my eyes jump up to meet his, where I see glimmer of amusement in them. I give him a look of annoyance and turn back to the screen, hoping he has no idea what I was actually looking at. Maybe he just saw I wasn't looking at the screen and was trying to get me to focus. I manage to get through the rest of the presentation without getting caught starring at any other body parts of my boss when the front desk clerk knocks on the door.

"Excuse me, Mr. Davis. Your food is here," he says as he holds up two large brown paper bags.

"Thank you, Aaron. You can leave it on the table over there."

James gets up and begins to pull out different containers of food, the smell instantly hitting me and making my stomach growl. When I get closer, I notice he is opening containers of pasta and breaded chicken.

"I hope you like Italian," he says.

"Are there really people out there who *don't* like Italian?"

He shrugs his shoulders. "You would be surprised."

We gather our plates and sit down at the table to eat. I spend the first couple minutes enjoying my food, before the silence gets to be too much for me.

"How often do you order in dinner at the office?" I ask.

"Probably more than I should. I don't really cook though so it would either be order in at my place or here. What about you?"

"If I work late, I am guilty of waiting to eat until I leave, even if it's nine. But I love to cook, so I eat fairly well when I don't work late or go out to dinner with friends."

He nods his head. "You seem like someone who goes out to dinner with friends a lot."

I can't tell if he means that as an insult, but I kind of think he might.

"I like to eat out with friends a decent amount. Is there something wrong with that?"

"No, I was thinking you seem like the type to."

Whatever, I don't even want to engage with him on this. It's just asking for us to begin fighting. I eat the rest of my food quickly so I can begin throwing out the garbage left on the table. James seems to think he has all day and I have to wait another ten minutes for him to finish. I'm waiting in my seat for him when he finally decides to join me.

"Did I do something to piss you off?" he asks as he plops back down in his chair.

"No, I'm just tired and want to get back to work."

"If you say so. I don't believe you but let's get back to it."

It's almost nine when we are done with all of the videos and have taken ours notes. If you want to hand me your notes, I will have Angela types both of ours up and organize it in a more helpful way. This is hours' worth of work. The control freak in me doesn't trust someone not to lose it, but I hand the notes over to him anyway. I pack up my things and agree to meet him in his office at nine tomorrow morning.

The morning has been extremely productive, we went over more of the processes that we are looking to improve in greater detail. Angela said she will have our notes organized for us by tomorrow morning. I don't know how she drops everything she has to do in order to meet this man's demands. I'm just about to head out of James' office when he stops me.

"What are your plans for lunch Peyton?"

I turn around slowly, caught off guard by the question.

"Oh um, I haven't really thought of it yet. I will probably just grab something at the corner café."

"Would you like to have lunch together?" he asks.

And that's why I am riding down the elevator right now with James, heading to the café to get lunch. Why did he ask me to lunch? That's the question I'm trying to answer as we enter the café. He doesn't come off as the type of boss who takes his employees out to lunch to get to know them. Hell, I've worked here for years, and he has barely acknowledged me. Nonetheless, I couldn't turn down lunch with the CEO of the company. I guess I have to grin and bear it.

We get seated quickly by an attractive waitress who seemed cozy with James. I have no doubt in my mind that James uses his good looks, wealth, and status to his advantage with the women in this city.

"Hello, Mr. Davis. How are you doing today?" The waitress confirms my suspicions that they know each other.

"I'm doing fine. Thank you for asking, Jody. How are you doing?"

"I'm great. What can I get for you two today?"

"I'll take the chicken salad sandwich with the pasta salad on the side and a water. Do you need a minute to look over the menu?" he turns to me.

"No, I'll have the roasted turkey sandwich with a side salad and a water as well."

Jody takes our orders and promises to be back shortly with our food. James leans his elbows on the table.

"So, Peyton. Tell me about yourself."

"What would you like to know?"

"Anything. I don't know much about you." *Whose fault is that?*

"Not much to know. I'm from Chicago. went to DePaul. I have three brothers, we all live locally here in the city."

"Three brothers? What was that like growing up?"

I smile at the memories. "Loud. Intense. I had to fight to get a word in or defend myself against their antics. They're all older than me."

smirks.

I never thought I would see the day that James' mouth would lift up in any sort of a smile. I mean it wasn't a full grin, but close enough.

"What does that mean?"

"Well, you certainly seem to hold your own. It makes sense now that you needed to do that growing up."

"Yeah, I suppose so. I never really thought about it like that. I have always been able to speak up for myself. I'm not afraid to say what needs to be said."

"That is a refreshing characteristic." I give him a look of shock. "What?"

"Did you just offer me a compliment?"

"Yes, I guess I did."

I smile from ear to ear at hearing him admit it.

"Don't let it go to your head. It was one compliment. More of an observation," he defends

"Uh uh! You're not getting out of it. You gave me a compliment and *can't* take it back. In fact, let's talk *more* about it. You think my ability to interject my opinion is refreshing. I'll make sure to remind you of that when you are rolling your eyes at me."

He chuckles. "Glad I said something."

My stomach flutters. There is something special about watching this man laugh with me for the first time. I feel like I just opened a present on Christmas morning. Somehow, we seemed to have broken through a barrier with each other. My nerves and discomfort are starting to fade away. As nice as that is, it also feels dangerous to see this man in any other way than intimidating. It's one thing for me to be intimidated in a business format. I have trained myself to still offer my opinion despite feeling intimidated. It's almost a requirement as a woman in a business setting surrounded by men.

"Tell me about yourself," I say to try to take the focus off of me for a second.

His mouth falls back into a grimace and serious Jameson is back. *What did I say wrong?*

"Not much to tell."

"Well, that can't be true. No one makes it to where you are at your age without something to tell."

"My parents died when I was young. I had to work hard to get into college. Worked even harder in college and have not stopped since."

"I'm sorry to hear about your parents. That must have been tough. I can only imagine how much hard work you had to put in to get where you are at today."

He shrugs his shoulders as if it was no big deal. Luckily, our food comes and offers a much-needed distraction. We eat and continue the rest of the lunch discussing the project. Whatever barrier I thought we had broken seems back in place. I guess he doesn't want me to ask any question about him. I get the feeling he has been through a lot in his twenty-eight years of life. Losing both your parents at a young age is already a lot for a kid. Somehow, I feel like that's not all there is to his story. I wonder how many people know the real Jameson Davis.

Once we're done and back at the office, we say goodbye and part ways to our offices with plans to meet the same time and place tomorrow morning.

I proceed to spend the rest of the workday gathering information for tomorrow. I got a lot done, despite my brain continuing to wander off to thoughts about James. He is such a mystery to me. This afternoon, I got glimpses of a man who can laugh and be carefree. There is something holding him back. I want to know what that is.

It's almost six by the time I call it quits. I have plans to have dinner with my brother Liam. He and his wife Becca are expecting a baby. It's the first baby in the family, we are all over the moon. When I walk into the restaurant, Liam calls my name and waves me over. He stands and gives me a big bear hug. I'll never tire of his over-the-top embraces.

"Hey, Pey Pey! How's it going?"

"It's going good, Lee! How's Becca and my future niece or nephew?" I ask as we take our seats.

His face is beaming at just the mention of them.

"They're great! We have an ultrasound coming up. Thank God Becca agreed to finally find out the sex. I told her she would struggle with setting up the nursery not knowing. It only took eight months for her to realize I was right."

"I can't wait! I have been dying to start shopping for my little nugget!"

"Mom hasn't been able to control herself. We are already stocked up on enough gender-neutral clothes for three babies." He says this like he is bothered but a small smile splays across his lips.

"Give her a break. She is about to become a *grandma*. It's her dream come true!"

"I know! I still cannot believe it."

We take our time looking over the menu and place our orders when the waitress comes over. We spend the time waiting for our food, joking around with each other. Things have always been so easy with us.

"So, how is work going?" he asks as we are digging into our dinner.

"It's going pretty good. Lance told me this week that he se-lected me to head up a large project for the company. I'll be working with the CEO to select a new ERP system. It's a great opportunity."

"That's great, Peyton! I'm proud of you. You're going to be the boss in no time."

"We will see about that. I have to impress James, the CEO, first. He's not easily impressed. Especially not with me."

"I don't believe a word of that. You're always working your ass off and you are crazy smart. There's nothing to not be impressed with."

"We will see. Right now, I'm just going to try to focus on the project and getting it done right. Hopefully, the work will speak for itself."

"Good attitude, sis."

After dinner, we walk outside, where we hug and say our goodbyes. Liam works downtown but commutes from a neighborhood close by. Becca insisted on finding a nice home outside of the city when they were trying for a baby. It's a perfect house, even if it is a little inconvenient for Liam to get to and from work.

It's only a fifteen-minute walk back to my place from here, and since it's a nice night out, I decide to walk home. The wind blows through the buildings, offering a nice breeze to cool me off from the summer heat. I think back to my lunch with James today. The moment I saw a glimmer of a real person. He has a beautiful smile. I can't imagine what it would be like to always be on the receiving end of that from him. I get the feeling he keeps that part of himself locked up more often than not. I hope tomorrow will offer some more glimpses into that side of him.

Chapter Four

James

Peyton walks into my office with a fresh smile on her face. The sun is shining in from the east windows, offering a glow behind her as she walks towards me. My heart starts to race, and my body instantly takes notice. It doesn't help when she gets closer, and I see the gray fitted dress she has on with tall, tan heels. The dress offers me a peek of her hourglass figure and my dick takes notice. I adjust myself under my desk when anger starts to rise. *Is she trying to kill me wearing that dress?*

"Morning, boss! Ready to get started?" She smiles and hands me a coffee. "Angela told me your favorite."

I scowl as I take the coffee from her. This isn't the kind of reaction I should be having towards an employee and it's all her fault for dressing like that.

"Let's get to work," I grumble as I walk past her to the conference table.

"Gee, thanks for picking up coffee for me, Peyton. No problem, James. It was my pleasure." She mimics as she follows me to the table, taking a seat next to me. I give her my best *I am not amused* expression.

"Can we just cut the attitude and get to work?"

"Yes, I would love it if *you* cut the attitude so we can get to work."

My head falls back in frustration at this woman.

"How about we start with reading through these reports sent over from finance. I'd like to see what type of information they are currently working with."

I ignore her remark and take a seat.

"You need to sit here; I do not have two copies of these reports."

When she takes a seat, I spread the reports across the table, and we get to work analyzing the data. There is so much here that it's almost too much for your brain to comprehend. Eventually, I see a trend in the reports and can spot a lot of the same information in different reports.

"I wonder why they have five different reports with the some of the same columns giving the same information," I point out.

Peyton looks over the information I am referencing. She stands up, leaning across me, to get a better look one of the reports farthest from her. I look at her concentrating as she takes it all in. I can see her braining spinning as she works to make sense of the information.

"Ah," she stands up straight. "It looks like these reports are sorting this information differently. Some of the reports must not be able to pull in from certain parts of the general ledger, leaving them to have to manipulate the data several different ways to get all the information that they need."

When I glance back at the spreadsheets, I can see what she is talking about.

"You're right, nice find. So, we need to figure out exactly why this information can't pull in automatically for them. Let's set up a meeting with all of the managers tomorrow. We can put together a list of questions that we need them to answer. I'll have Angela set it up. What does your schedule look like tomorrow?"

"Well, seeing as that you made me relinquish all of my prior duties, I'm available whenever you need me."

"Is it possible for you to answer me without that sarcastic undertone?" I stand up with her.

She giggles at my frustration. "Sorry, boss. I guess you just bring it out of me."

"Gee, lucky me."

I walk towards my desk to put in my call to Angela before I forget. What she doesn't notice is the smile I let loose when my back is to her.

After my phone call, I sit down at my desk and rub my eyes. The hours worked at this company can sometimes catch up with me at the most random times. When I look back at Peyton, she's watching me with a curious eye.

"You alright?" she asks as she walks over to my side of the desk, leaning her hip on the edge.

"Yeah, sorry. Must not have gotten good sleep last night."

I shake my head in an effort to wake myself up.

"Anything I can do to help? I can go pick up some lunch for you, grab you some coffee, maybe even be nice for the rest of the week."

I can't help but laugh quietly at her dig on herself. "It's Friday, Peyton. That's hardly an accomplishment when we have an hour left of our meetings for the week."

"Hey, take it or leave it," she shrugs.

"Okay," I sigh. "I'll take a coffee and your kindness for the next hour."

She nods her head and starts for the door. I catch her before she is out of sight.

"Hey!" I say, she turns around. "Thank you."

Chapter Five

Peyton

"Okay, so hear me out before you freak out," I say to my friend Blake.

She is recently divorced and just moved into her new house. I asked her to come spend the night with me since it's the weekend. A couple of my friends want to check out this exclusive club that turns into a sex club of sorts once a month. It's definitely something none of us have ever done, but we thought it was a good idea over a couple of bottles of wine last weekend. It's very exclusive but Janet knows the owner who has been trying to convince her to give it a shot for months now.

"Coming from you, Peyton, that scares me." She isn't lying. I'm known as the crazy one between the two of us. So, for me to start off like that, she knows it must be something completely insane.

"So, Janet knows this guy who owns Club Toxic."

"Okkkay. That doesn't sound so bad. You want to check it out tonight?"

"Yes! Janet, Melissa, and I wanted to check it out tonight. Only.... tonight, may be a bit...different than other nights."

Oh god, how am I going to get her to agree to this?

"Different *how* exactly?

"So, it turns into more of a sex club. But we don't have to....," I don't even get to finish my sentence.

"Are you crazy? Peyton, have you lost your *mind*? There is no way we are going to a sex club."

finish, you would have let me explain that we are not going there to *do* anything. We're just going to check it out. See what happens at a place like that. It's like an adventure."

"Omg, Peyton! If you want an adventure, go sky diving or something."

"Come on! It'll be fun. We can drink and pretend we are in some old movie from the fifties."

"What exactly do you think happened in clubs in the fifties, Peyt?"

"I don't know! But when I think of a sex club, I think of that era." I begin pouring a glass of wine for each of us. I think she will need alcohol to get the nerve to do this. "Either way, that's beside the point. We're going tonight. I don't care if I have to drag you in. You have been moping around here for the last couple months, and I get it, but it's time to let loose and have some fun."

"We are *just* going to observe and judge?" She gives me a skeptical eye.

"Of course. Who do you think I am?

"I can't believe I'm agreeing to this. I must have lost my mind, along with my future."

Honestly, the fact that she agreed that quickly is shocking, but I'm going with it. I drag her into my room and tell her that I'm dressing her. After ten minutes of arguing, she agrees to a little black dress that shows off her assets. I settle on a dark red dress that hangs low in the front, with a length that cuts off a couple inches below my bottom. I don't want to look out of place, that will probably draw in *more* attention.

We agree to meet Janet and Melissa outside of the club around ten. So, after we are both ready to hit the town, I drab a reluctant Blake out the door at quarter to ten.

"Hey ladies! Looking good!" Janet whistles as we get out of the car.

"Who is ready for a wild night?" Melissa suggests. Blake gives me an eye that means *it better not be too wild or I will kill you.*

We make our way into the club after fifteen minutes of waiting for Janet's friend to let the bouncer know we are good. They are very serious about being on the list. As we enter, the lighting is dim with red lights offering a seductive feel to the atmosphere. Smoke seems to be floating around the air, making some areas of the room appear out of nowhere the closer you get. There are women dressed in lingerie walking around with champagne. We all snatch a glass and guzzle the drink, as if we are hoping the champagne will provide us with the courage to continue. I look to my left and see a couple in the corner of the room having sex. The woman is on top, straddling the male and going at it. Holy shit!

"Oh shit, guys look to your left right now!" I mutter. Everyone turns to the left and whip their head back around to me like they were not supposed to be looking. I laugh at their reactions. "I think it's okay to look guys. It seems like they want that. I mean, it's kind of hot."

Melissa turns her head back around and a slow smile creeps up on her face. "It is kind of hot," she agrees.

Blake looks like she has seen a ghost. I nudge her arm to catch her attention. "Loosen up girl. Remember it's just for fun. You aren't going to be doing anything yourself."

Once we get to the bar, we grab some drinks to get the night started. I order a round of shots to take first to further loosen us up. When I slam the shot glass down, I look out into the crowd. There are women half dressed, tops off, making out with men or other women. You name it, it's likely happening right now. There are curtains pulled back behind me, leading to another section of the club.

"Let's go check out the rest of the place first," I tell the girls.

Realizing I need to lead the way since everyone else seems to be paralyzed with shock. I laugh as I head past the curtains and down a hallway. The hallway opens up to a large room with chandeliers hanging from the ceilings. There are four wooden corner bars in each corner of the room with men in bow ties mixing drinks. A band is playing Sinatra while couples are dancing on the wooden dance floor. I turn to Blake with victory in my eyes.

"Ah ha! Look at this place! It is like we went back in time to the fifties." She rolls her eyes at me.

We walk around the room, taking in the scene. This seems like a much more sophisticated area of the club. There are several closed curtains along the walls of this large room. I wonder if that is where couples go for more privacy. We settle on a high-top table near the bar while we enjoy watching the band and chatting. After we order another round of drinks, I'm sipping my wine when I look across the room and see dark eyes staring at me. James Davis is looking at me with noticeable anger in his eyes. The men that he is standing with seem to notice the way he is looking at me and begin laughing. I look away, embarrassed by the sudden attention. When I steal a glance their way, I notice they are all heading towards our table except for James who moves on to talk to a woman near him.

"Shit! Don't look, but the guys that are approaching were just standing with my boss. I'm so screwed! I can't believe he has seen me here. He's going to think I'm a whore!"

The girls don't have time to react because the guys have already made it to our table.

"Hello, ladies," one of them says.

They are all ridiculously attractive, wearing expensive suits that fit in a way that makes you want to rip them off to see what is hiding underneath.

"Hello yourself," Janet replies.

"We haven't seen you around here before. Is this your first time?"

"I know the owner. We are more spectators than participants," Janet clarifies.

I see Blake instantly relax now that they know not to expect anything from us. I smile at her reaction.

"No shame in watching. Sometimes that can be just as fun. I'm Jackson," he introduces himself.

Everyone goes around the table introducing themselves as the guys stay and make conversation. They are actually extremely polite and before we know it, we are all laughing and having a good time. Even Blake has eased up enough to join in on the conversation. I can't help but steal glances at James from across the room. Every time I do, he is looking at me with the same intense stare. I really hope he doesn't let seeing me here affect our working relationship. Although, he seems to come here all the time. I can tell by how comfortable he is. That must mean he participates. A wave of jealousy shoots through my veins at the thought of him behind the curtains with another woman. Has he been with the blonde bombshell that he is talking with right now? They look comfortable in each other's presence.

When the band starts up with another song, Jackson turns to Janet and asks her if she would like to dance. Next thing I know, they are dragging all of us out on the dance floor.

We dance and sway in their arms, as they twirl us around the dance floor.

"What's your name again?" my guy asks with a silly grin on his face. "Sorry, I'm terrible at remembering names."

I laugh out loud at his admission. "Don't worry about it. I have no clue what your name is. Mine's Peyton."

"I'm Greg."

The music switches tune to a faster song and before I know it, Greg and I are moving our hips to the beat. When I look over to James, he's gone. My heartbeat accelerates at the thought of him moving to a more private area with that blonde. My imagination can't take me any further because a hand is grabbing my arm and pulling me away from Greg. I turn to see James staring at me with such intensity that I start to feel heat gathering in my core.

"Greg, go find someone else to dance with," James barks while still holding my eyes.

Greg laughs and backs away with his hands up in surrender. I feel shocked and humiliated that he thought he can come over here and decide who I can dance with. I turn around to storm off when he grips my arm again and swings me around.

"Where do you think you're going?" he questions.

"Away from you!" I try to get out of his hold, but he latches on tighter.

"What? I'm not a good enough dancing partner?" he says as he moves his hands to my hips and pulls me forward, beginning to move to the music.

"Maybe if you came up and asked for a dance like a normal person! Not demanding my partner leave me like I'm your property."

He chuckles. "Greg is not wounded; don't you worry about him. Plus, I was saving you. He is here for one thing only, and trust me, you don't want it."

"Maybe I do." I protest as he continues moving us about the dance floor like he doesn't even have to think. "Where did you learn to dance like this?"

"Foster parents were into ballroom dancing. They insisted I learn."

He meets my eyes and glides his hands up my waist just to slide them back down. I'm stunned into silence at his admission about foster care. I remember him telling me his parents died young. I figured a grandparent or aunt and uncle raised him.

"I didn't know you were a foster child. I'm sorry," I whisper.

"Not many people do. It's not information I give out freely." My heart skips a beat knowing he is trusting this information with me. "Now tell me, why are you here?"

"Why are *you* here?"

"Don't play with me, Ms. Brady. You work for my company, and I have a right to know what one of my employees is doing at a place like this."

I cannot believe he thinks he can judge me for being at the same place he is. What a hypocrite!

"*Mr.* Davis, are you judging me for attending this type of event for the *first* time, while it appears that you are very familiar with this scene?" He stares at me with a look that could cut through glass as his hands squeeze my sides, hard. Reality sets in and the desire to keep my job hits me with force.

"My friend knows the owner. We were just curious what it was like and wanted to see for ourselves. We have no intention of participating in anything."

An audible breath is released from him as he relaxes into me. I can almost feel his anger begin to dissipate. "But I could participate if I wanted to, I'll have you know."

"And do you want to?"

"I...I'm not sure. I guess I don't even know much about it."

The song comes to an end and James lets go of me, still hanging on to one of my hands as he tells me to follow him.

"Where are we going?" I ask.

"You said you don't know much about these events; I'm going to show you around." He turns around with a smirk on his face. "That is unless you don't want to learn more about it."

"I thought you didn't want one of your employees at a place like this?" I can't help the sarcastic tone that oozes out of my mouth. He gives me a watchful eye before replying.

"Well, seeing as you are already here, I might as well show you around. As long as this stays between us." I nod my head in understanding. We each have a reputation to protect at work.

He leads me through the hallway back to the main room. We move around the bar until we are at the back of the room where there are couches scattered around the perimeter of the room. I look around and see there are people kissing and grinding on each other in every direction that I look. Male on male, male on female, female on female, threesomes, you name it. My eyes do a double take on a man sitting naked while a woman rides him with her back to his stomach. There is another male on his knees between them going down on the woman while all this is happening. I don't even understand how they are accomplishing this. I feel heat pull in my stomach and spread down.

"Do you like what you see, Peyton?" James pulls me out of my trance and shame fills me at being caught staring. I tilt my head down to hide the warmth spreading across my cheeks. James steps in front of me, puts his hand under my chin, and pulls my face up to meet his. "Don't ever feel ashamed for what turns you on. This place is a guilt free zone. It's here for your pleasure."

I nod my head at him. I never knew I had this side to me. A side that could enjoy watching others being intimate. I realize how bad this looks that I discover this with my boss at my side. I can only hope that we are able to put this behind us, but tonight I'm going to let myself enjoy.

"Do these people know each other?"

"Sure, some of them do. Some are couples who come here to be watched. Others are strangers just looking for a no strings attached evening. This is more of the exhibitionist room, that is why there are no privacy curtains."

"What's the room we were in?" I ask hesitantly.

"That's where you can enjoy live music while drinking and smoking some cigars. It's for people that are looking for a classier evening that could end with someone else. There are no public acts aloud in that room, which is why you see so many private areas along the back wall."

"What do you prefer?"

"That's a bit of a personal question now, isn't it?" he smirks down at me making my insides spread with desire.

Flirty James is a lethal combination with his good looks and confidence.

"I'm sorry. That was inappropriate of me to ask." I flush from embarrassment.

"Come on. There is still one more level."

He grabs my hand once again and escorts me to a stairwell in the back. As we climb, the pulsing erotic music playing downstairs fades away.

Chapter Six

James

The feel of her small hand in mine gives my body sensations that I have no business feeling. Not only is she my employee, but she is far too good to be with a man like myself. I closed the door on relationships a long time ago. Which is the very reason I come to a place like this in the first place. It gives me a chance to meet someone who will not have any expectations outside of a night together. I learned a while ago not to trust a woman when she told me she wasn't looking for anything serious. Spend enough intimate nights together, and they are always looking for more.

I know I'm going to hell for interacting with Peyton at all in this environment. She's too good for this place, even if she is only here as an observer like she says she is. When I saw her, I could not help the rage that filled inside of me. The thought of her here with another man created a fury I wasn't sure I would be able to suppress. Thankfully, I was able to calm down when she told me she wasn't here for the reasons I had assumed. As her boss, doing anything except leaving immediately after I noticed her is completely inappropriate. Yet as I walk up the stairs with her hand in mine, I can't find it in myself to turn around.

As we approach the top of the steps, I stop to figure out which way we should go when she bumps into me. The feel of her body pressed against mine sends shivers down by back and makes my pants feel tight. I hear an audible gasp as her other hand grabs the front of my shirt, presumably to prevent herself from falling back. She doesn't remove her hand right away. Instead, she lingers there before slowly lowering it down my stomach until she lets go. It felt more like a caress down my body than someone who just needed to catch themselves from falling backward. Before I do something that I will regret, I begin walking to the right, dragging her along with me. I find a bar in the corner and pick two seats for us to sit in while she still stands, taking everything in. Confusion seems to set in as her face scrunches up. I try to hide my smirk as I look at her analyzing the crowd, trying to decipher what is playing out in front of her.

"Umm, I'm confused." She looks at me and must notice the amusement written all over my face. "You can wipe that grin off your face first. Then, you can explain to me what exactly is going on."

I chuckle at her sassiness. No woman has ever had the nerve to talk to me like that, especially none that work for me. Sometimes I think she forgets that I hold her future in my hands. I like that more than I should. "What do you think is going on?"

"What do I think is going on? I think there are a bunch of couples eating dinner in a fancy restaurant. Is downstairs the only entrance to this place or is there some kind of side or back entrance?"

"You can only get here the way we came, Peyton."

"Sooo, people just walk straight through a sex club up to... this?"

"Yes, they do actually," I smirk.

"Cut the shit and give me some more insight here. There is no way a restaurant would willingly choose this location."

My body reacts to the way she spoke to me, the way she is not intimated to put me in my place. There is only so long I can tolerate her attitude before I break and do something I will regret. I hope she doesn't see the real reason I'm angry, that its anger at wanting to shut her mouth with my own. She shifts in her seat, looking slightly ashamed of her boldness. I finally decide to put her out of her misery.

"Some people don't want to feel like they met someone at a club to have sex. It can feel cheap and impersonal. So, they come here and put their names in for a companion to join them for dinner. If they click, they are free to continue to use the rest of the club as much as they desire. If they don't, hopefully they at least enjoyed a good conversation over a great meal."

She takes a moment to look around the room, taking everything in. There are crystal chandeliers hanging from the ceiling, offering a dim light for a more intimate setting. The wait staff are all dressed in black and are attractive and appealing to the eyes. It helps to get in the mood when you have something delicious to look at.

"I'm not sure I understand. Why not just go on a real date? Why come *here*?"

"Because Peyton, some people don't want to have to worry about whether or not their date is going to feel used if they know all you are looking for is sex. Or if they claim that's all they want, when they are just hoping you change your mind along the way. You are more likely to find someone who is only after the same things as you when you are at a place like this. It takes the stress away from it all."

"I didn't know people found it that difficult to find someone to...spend *time* with without it turning into something more. Just go to a bar, I see it all the time."

"You would be surprised," I whisper under my breathe.

"Is that why you come here?"

"I'm too busy for a relationship," I shrug. "This makes it easier for me. I don't have to court anyone or worry about misleading them." She nods while taking in my response. I appreciate that she doesn't seem to judge me.

"Would you like a drink?" I nod to the bar behind us.

She bites her bottom lip as she contemplates her answer. "Sure. Cabernet for me, please."

"A cab for the lady and a bourbon for me."

The bartender nods in response and gets to work on our drinks. When I hand her the glass, she takes a big gulp. I wonder if she is nervous about where she is or that she is here with me.

"Hey," I wait until she looks at me. "I want you to know this does not change anything between us at work. I would never judge you for coming here, I was just surprised."

She offers a smile and tension seems to fall off her in waves. "Thank you! And just so you know, I don't judge you either."

"I appreciate that!" She has no idea what that means to me.

"So, enough of this awkwardness. Let's talk about something else. Like why Owen from marketing is always whistling as he walks around the office. And why you haven't fired him for annoying the crap out of everyone on our floor."

I laugh. "I didn't know that Owen is always whistling. I will report it to HR immediately so we can have a sit-down meeting about that type of inappropriate behavior. Now you can do me a solid and tell Tricia to stop following me around when I come to your floor. She is there at every turn I make, smiling at me!"

"Oh my gosh! What?" I crack up. "Tricia is the absolute worst! She is always talking about her dates with wealthy assholes around the city. Stay away from that one!"

"Trust me, I try."

I'm surprised at how much fun I am having with her. I have completely forgot about the real reason I came here as we continue to laugh about the office quirks. After we finish our drinks, we decide to head back downstairs to find our friends. I was hoping to come here to blow off some much-needed steam tonight and get my head straight. Now, I fear that sharing this with her just made it impossible for me to control these feelings. The next few months are going to be torture.

When I get into work on Monday, I'm greeted by my friend, Greg, who works in the same building. We met in college and have remained friends ever since. He is one of the only people who knows about my past, and I haven't even shared all of it with him. Some things are better left buried away where they belong.

"Hey man! It's about time you got your lazy ass into work." He remains seated in my chair like he owns the place.

"Fuck off! You beat me to work one day and all of a sudden you are Mr. Responsible. Now get the fuck out of my chair." He laughs before finally surrendering and moving to one of the chairs across from my desk.

"What's on the agenda for today? Anything I'll give a crap about?"

"Probably nothing you would care about. Just meeting with our Director of IT to continue looking into new ERP systems. It'll likely eat up most of my day. I really want to get this thing off the ground as soon as possible." An image of Greg and Peyton dancing together on Saturday night hits me and I panic at the thought of the two of them running into each other. The last thing that I want is for Greg to realize I work with her. I'll never hear the end of it, especially since he wouldn't quit asking me where we disappeared to that night and if I got any action. "Now if you don't mind, I need to get a few things done before she arrives."

"No worries. I'll head out soon."

"No, get the fuck out *now*!"

He looks at me like I'm crazy. Probably because I am acting crazy right now. I'm a dick, but I don't typically kick him out of my office the second I arrive. Just as I'm about to drag him out of my office, Peyton walks in with her bag slung over her shoulder and a bright smile on her face.

"Oh, sorry, I didn't mean to interrupt. I can wait outside." She begins to reverse when Greg turns around. I can see the moment recognition hits her face and she trips over herself before holding onto the doorframe.

"No need to leave on my account," Greg interjects before she makes it out of the office. "Just two friends catching up before work here, nothing important." He turns to me with a cocky smirk on his face. "She looks familiar, James. Have we met before?"

"Get. Out. Now!" I say between clenched teeth.

He barks out a laugh as he stands up. I see Peyton put her head down while he passes by, as if she can hide from the embarrassment.

"You two behave now," the bastard says before he walks out of the office.

"Ignore him, Peyton. I'm still waiting for him to grow up but have stopped holding my breath. It doesn't seem to be happening anytime soon."

Luckily, she lets out a giggle as she sits down, which seems to have broken the tension.

"So, I was doing some more research on this DRN company. I think they are the front runner in my mind. They seem to have all the features we are looking for, a competitive price, and offer a great staff of consultants that'll work with us in person until everything is up and running."

"You think they would be able to fulfill the needs of everyone in finance including the tax department?" I ask.

"Within reason. Look, no software is going to transition perfectly into any company structure. We will need to bend a bit
and accept some change in our processes. The consultants
will be here to work with us along the way to make sure we are
using the system to its full capabilities. But if we are looking
at the big picture, they fulfill everything we're looking for."

I can't help but feel like she is so sexy when she talks to me like
that. An image of her dancing at the club pops into my head.
She felt so good in my arms. How will I ever forget the look of
desire on her face when she was watching the two men have
sex with another woman? Her arousal was so apparent. My
dick begins to grow in my pants. Minutes must have passed by
with me lost in thought because she clears her throat, offering
me raised eyebrows, waiting for my response.

"Oh, ugh... okay. Let's go over their features and why you think
they are the front runner so far."

We spend the next couple of hours running through everything until I hear her stomach growl. She looks slightly embarrassed with herself for being caught. I can't help but chuckle
at her bashful look. She is just so charming when she tries
to portray herself a certain way, when I know she is just a
wild, carefree spirit. I admire her tenacity. She knows what
she wants out of her career and how she wants to be treated,
and she will settle for nothing less.

"I think your stomach is telling us to call it a day." She bites
her bottom lip, trying to hide her smirk. I move on quickly to
avoid further embarrassment for her. "This is a great start so
far. Let's plan on trying to schedule a meeting with DRN for
a presentation on their system as soon as possible. I will have
Angela set that up for us. I think we should still move forward
with TSR as well. I would like to see them go head-to-head
and sell their product to us."

"I agree."

She begins packing her things as we plan to meet up again
tomorrow with some other managers to go over some other
processes that we need to have a better grasp on. I pull out
my phone to buzz Greg to see what he is doing for lunch. I

need to bust his ass and make sure he doesn't plan on coming around anymore just to make Peyton feel uncomfortable.

He lets me know he can meet me at our go-to restaurant in twenty minutes. I get there before him to make sure we get a seat.

"Hey man. Hope you weren't waiting too long," he says as he shrugs off his suit jacket.

"Nah, not at all."

We put our orders in and begin catching each other up on work. He's the district attorney here in the city. It's no small undertaking. The stress and responsibility can often get to him. I know that is likely the reason why he is so closed off and unwilling to settle down. He never knows when a big case will come his way and demand all of his time and attention. He is as immature as they come, but don't let that fool you when it comes to his abilities. He's damn good at what he does. I think the severity of his work is why he lets loose.

"Speaking of the new software search...you neglected to tell me that the beauty from the other night that you cock blocked me from was your Director of IT."

"I hardly think that I cock blocked you, it was one dance." I grip my glass to try to control the rage building inside of me at the thought of Greg with Peyton. I hate my reaction to this woman. This is not me; I am always in control of my emotions.

"Whatever you say. Care to tell me what is going on between the two of you?"

"There's nothing going on between us. She is my employee; you know nothing could happen. Not that I want anything to happen."

Greg laughs and hits the table with his hand. "That's a good one man. Keep telling yourself that. Any idiot can see how much you too want each other. Anyway, who cares if she is your employee, she is management. I think you should go for it. I haven't seen you this way with anyone since Margaret. You clearly like her."

"I told you before to never bring up that woman ever again."

"Are you really never going to tell me what happened between the two of you? One day you are engaged and happy, the next I can't even bring up her name."

"It doesn't matter what happened. I already told you it's not worth a discussion, end of story."

"I'm just trying to understand you, man. You go around acting like nothing bothers you, like you are happy pushing everyone away, but you're the only one falling for your own act."

He thinks this is an act? No, I'm very content not letting anyone into my world. No one wants to be a part of a dark past and someone filled with such flaws. Just like my ex-fiancé told me, *you will never be able to give a woman everything she needs*, and she was right. I'm fundamentally broken and can't be enough for anyone.

We manage to keep the rest of the lunch free of self-improvement discussions, yet I do not feel like Greg has any interest in letting the topic remain buried.

When I arrive back at the office, Angela is sitting at her desk on the phone and holds up a finger for me to wait. I would normally get annoyed if someone expects me to stand there and wait for them to finish their discussion, like my time isn't valuable. However, I know Angela and she wouldn't stop me unless it was something important.

"Okay, thank you for your time. I appreciate all your help," she says. "Uh huh, goodbye."

She hangs up the phone and I raise my eyebrows, waiting for her to speak.

"Okay, that was DRN. They can't make it to Chicago anytime in the next three weeks to do a presentation."

I become visibly annoyed, as I purse my lips together and my back stiffens. We don't have three weeks to wait for them to get here. That will throw off our entire deadline.

"BUT," Angela continues. "They did have a last-minute cancellation for a presentation at their office in New York City this Thursday. They're willing to give you this spot if you will go to New York."

"Okay, I'll take it. We really do not have much of a choice at this point. Please inform Peyton of the presentation and book our accommodations."

"Absolutely, I'll get right on it," she turns to her computer.

"Thank you."

As I walk away, I realize I will be stuck spending the night in the same hotel as Peyton. This is the last thing that I need, picturing her naked in her hotel shower right next to mine. I let out a low groan at the thought of having to endure this trip.

Chapter Seven

Peyton

"Becca, you're the most beautiful pregnant woman I have ever seen."

"Oh, stop it, Peyton. You can tell me the truth; I'm a cow," Becca replies while rubbing her belly.

"It's no use, Peyton. I always compliment how gorgeous she looks carrying my child. She never takes the compliment well." My brother Liam complains while we are sitting outside on their back patio.

It was a long week of work and dealing with James' hot and cold behavior. One minute he is acting normal and even pleasant with me, the next he does a complete one-eighty and becomes cold and demanding. I can't pretend that I haven't wondered what that demanding side of him is like in the bedroom. I have found myself thinking of what he does with the women in the club. Does he tell them what to do and get rough with them? I may have pictured him doing those things to me when I'm alone at night and can't control where my brain takes me. Becca snaps me out of my thoughts.

"I would accept those compliments if I thought there was any truth to them."

"Whatever! You guys can argue all you want; I just can't believe we are weeks away from getting to meet the nugget. How are you feeling?"

"Honestly, all things considered, I feel pretty good. This has been a relatively easy pregnancy. I'm, however, looking forward to it being over. I can't wait to become a mom."

Liam leans over and gives Becca a kiss on the cheek. "You're going to be an amazing mom."

"Ugh, you guys are so cute it almost makes me sick," I reply in feign jealousy. In reality, Becca and Liam are my relationship goals. They support each other and challenge each other in the best way.

We have already finished eating brunch and are just enjoying the weather and each other's company. I wanted to get a visit in before they are busy figuring out parenthood.

"Peyton, Liam tells me you are killing it at work. How's this new project going?"

"It's going pretty good. We're flying to New York City this week for a presentation from one of the software companies on our list."

"A trip to New York sounds amazing! Hopefully you get some free time to enjoy the city," Becca says.

"I wish! I'm sure James will have us working nonstop. He is obsessed with getting this project moving at the speed of light."

"Oh, please. After work hours at least, you will have time to explore. Ugh, it's going to be years before we get to take a trip," she says as she rubs her belly.

"You act like you won't have all of her family begging to babysit," I remind her.

"You're right. I guess as we get closer, I'm becoming more aware of how much our life is going to change."

Becca and I sit out on the lounge chairs and enjoy the rest of the evening as we let the warmth of the setting sun wrap us up like a blanket. We talk about how excited but nervous she's about becoming a mom. I assure her that she's going to be an amazing mom, and I mean it. She's so patient and loving with my brother, you can tell that will pour over into motherhood. Liam and I come from a very close-knit family. Having babies starting to join the family is all anyone can talk about. After saying goodbye to Liam and Becca, I head home to pack for our trip to New York on Tuesday. I figure we could be working late tomorrow to prepare. Being packed and ready will assure I am not scrambling at the last minute and forgetting something.

It's Wednesday morning and I'm running around like a crazy person trying to make sure I'm ready. I knew this would happen. Even when I try to pack and prepare early, I am still running late. We worked until nine last night. I didn't get into bed until midnight after dinner and taking a shower. Now it's five am, and I need to be at the airport in thirty minutes. James will fire me on the spot if I miss my flight.

I'm actually running towards the gate with only minutes to spare. James is standing at the desk with an icy glare as I approach.

"Well, I'm glad you decided it was worth it to show up," he barks out.

"I'm.... soorr.... rry," I pant as I hand the lady my ticket.

"Just grab your bag and let's go." He nods at my luggage and takes off in front of me.

I grab my suitcase and speed walk to keep up with his pace. Once we board the airplane, we are shown to our seats by an attractive stewardess. She's not subtle about her attraction to James, and I feel a small twinge of jealousy rush through me. James lifts his luggage into the overhead bin and turns around with his hand out. I look down at it confused before I look up at him.

"What?"

"Your bag?" he says as he looks down at my luggage.

Mr. Nice and Helpful?" I ask in a mocking tone. Sometimes I can't help myself with him. He gives me his signature exasperated look and rolls his eyes at me.

"Just give me the damn bag, Peyton."

"Fine. Here you go." I offer it to him with a side of attitude and snatch the window seat. I'm sure first class is nothing new for him, but this could be one of the only times I experience this, so I'm taking full advantage. Luckily, he doesn't say anything and lets me take the seat.

We spend the majority of the flight in silence while he checks emails on his phone, and I listen to a podcast on mine. I look over at him and hear him grumble about something and move onto another email. Another sigh from him and I can't take it any longer, I pat him on the shoulder.

"Yes?" he looks at me like I interrupted a meeting with the shareholders.

"Do you ever stop working?" I ask him.

"Well, it is a workday and it's during work hours. Why wouldn't I be working?"

"Because you're on a plane. Do you really need to spend every waking second working? You need to learn to relax, maybe you will sleep better if you do."

I realize saying this to my boss isn't the smartest idea, but it would not kill him to lighten up and relax for a minute.

"Okay. And what are you listening to that's so much better than working?"⌷

"If you must know, I'm listening to a podcast. Right now, it's talking about some of Jimmy Fallon's best bits." He gives me an eye as if to say *is that really what you think is so interesting and funny?*

"Is that what you've been giggling about over there for the last hour?"

I giggle just thinking about it. "Yes. Here just take my other ear bud and listen for a minute. See if you spontaneously combust from not replying to an email within five seconds of receiving it."

"Fine," he grumbles but takes the ear bud.

We sit there for a couple minutes listening to some of the tweets from people talking about some of their most embarrassing moments. I cannot help but chuckle at some of them. I even catch James with a small grin on his face at some of them. When he catches me looking, his frown is back in place immediately. The host begins reading off a tweet about an employee getting caught falling asleep at their desk only to bow their head and say 'amen' when their boss walks by, in an effort to play it off like they were praying. My laughter cannot be contained as I imagine using this on Lance in the office. Much to my surprise, I look over at James to find his hand over his mouth as his shoulders begin to shake.

We look at each other and both begin to crack up. It does not take long before we are no longer laughing at the tweet so much as at each other's reaction. I have tears running down my cheeks by the time we contain ourselves. I begin wiping them away as I take out my earbud. James follows suit and gives mine back to me.

"What did you think?" I ask as I take it back from him. I try to ignore the electricity that shoots through me at the touch of his hand.

"Okay, so it was funny. I suppose there is some benefit to relaxing a bit on the plane," he says as I watch him try to gain back composure.

"Ah ha! He does have a sense of humor and he *can* relax."

"Gloating isn't an attractive quality, Ms. Brady."

"Are you saying you otherwise find me attractive?" I smile up at him.

He smiles back and winks at me and I swear my bodies almost has an orgasm right there. I just can't seem to help my attraction to him and watching him loosen isn't helping. It makes me want to throw myself at him. I never could resist an attractive, successful man who knows how to laugh and enjoy life. First impression would be that James has no clue how to relax, but I feel like I can get him to forget how to be serious all the time.

After we land, we make our way to the hotel to freshen up. We plan to meet up in the hotels business center to get some work done before our meeting in the morning. We fly out right after our meeting tomorrow, giving us just one night in the city. Once I have changed into jeans and an off the shoulder top, I grab my laptop and make my way downstairs. Not surprisingly, James is already down there working. I take a seat next to him and begin to connect to the Wi-Fi. I notice he's still in his business attire and can't help but roll my eyes.

"I can sense the attitude from a mile away, Peyton. What's your problem now?" he says while typing.

"It's just that...why are you dressed so professionally? We're just working in the hotel. We're not going to see anyone else but each other."

"I like to make a good impression wherever I go. You never know who you're going to run into or meet."

"Right. You plan on running into anybody in the business center of our hotel in New York City?"

"Crazier things have happened." He is looking into my eyes now like he is trying to convey some deeper meaning to what he said. Crazier things like a CEO having sex with his staff?

I shake off the ridiculous thoughts and hook up my computer to begin reviewing some of the spreadsheets I requested from managers. We work steadily side by side for a couple hours before I decide I need some lunch. I pull off my headphones and turn to him, waiting for a good time to interrupt. After several minutes, I decide he's either completely engrossed in his work and doesn't notice me or he is ignoring me. I find out it's the latter.

"Are you ready for lunch?" I question.

"Took you long enough to speak."

"What? You knew I was waiting for your attention the whole time? Why didn't you stop typing?" I ask all flustered and annoyed.

"I wanted to see how long you would hold out," he says with a smirk. At least he is lightening up a bit, even if it's at my expense.

"Well, congrats. You won! Now, can we go get something to eat please?"

"Ugh, fine! I was going to work through lunch, but I suppose if you're that hungry."

"Well, unlike you, I'm not a machine. I need sustenance to continue."

We pack up our things and put them behind the concierge and walk out onto the streets of New York. I look left and right at the bustling traffic. Even though we live in Chicago, New York has such a different feel to it. It's more intense. I look to James to see if he is going to lead the way.

"So, I've never actually been to New York. You know of some-where we can eat?"

He shrugs and takes my hand as he begins to weave through the crowd. He doesn't let go as we continue down the street. We only walk for about two blocks before we find a cute little café with outdoor seating. He heads up to the front and asks for a table outside. We settle into our seats and place our orders before we really begin speaking, he's the first to break the silence.

"So, never been to New York, huh?"

"Surprisingly, no. I never had business that brought me here and always wanted to travel some place warm for vacation. What about you?"

"I've been here plenty. Work has brought me here plenty of times, but I'm not sure I have ever been out to eat like this for lunch. Not unless we were taking a client out, but that's normally for dinner. Most of the time though, it's lunch and dinner in the hotel."

"What? You have never taken the time to explore New York? What's wrong with you?"

He chuckles at my admittedly over-the-top reaction. Come on though, who travels to New York that many times and doesn't take *some* time to explore?

"There's a lot wrong with me. Are you just seeing that now?" he says over a bite of salmon.

"I guess you hide it well." I wink at him and get another laugh in response. We spend the rest of lunch enjoying the weather, food, and to my surprise, pleasant conversation.

When we get back to the hotel, it's straight back to work. He wastes no time whipping out his laptop. I think I last about two hours before my mind is drifting to all the things that are outside waiting for me to see. It's three o'clock now, there's plenty of daylight left to explore the city. I'm trying to come up with the best way to approach James about calling it a day and seeing the city. I suppose I could just go out and see it myself, but it would be more enjoyable with someone else. I have seen him relax a couple times, but he is still my boss and a workaholic. I would still be basically asking my boss to play hooky with me. After several minutes, I work up the courage to say something.

"So, you've really never explored the city while you were here?" I scooch around in my seat while asking, nervous for what his reaction is going to be.

"Not really." He turns his head to look at me with a questioning eyebrow. I can feel that he is just waiting for me to say it.

"It's such a beautiful day. I've never been here before. It would be such a shame for me to leave tomorrow without seeing anything. My brother will be asking me what I saw when I was here. I would hate to tell him I didn't have time to see anything. And my sister-in-law...," he cuts me off before I can continue.

"If we do some sightseeing and go out to dinner, will you stop talking?"

I can't help but break out into a huge smile. "Yes! Yes! I promise I will."

He gets back to typing while I sit there bouncing my knees and fidgeting.

Chapter Eight

James

I have every intention of taking her out to see the city, but I can't help but make her sweat a bit. I take my time responding to my final email as I see her bouncing around in her seat next to me. I'm not sure why I have never explored the city. Honestly, I've never even considered it. She makes it sound like I'm the crazy one, yet she is the one bouncing around like a little kid about to enter a candy store.

"Okay, last email is sent. Let's go see New York before you have an aneurysm."

"Yes! Let's go!"

She is out of her chair with our bags within seconds of my announcing that I'm done. Once we hit the sidewalk, she turns to me with a smile does something to me. It makes me feel less... *angry* at the world.

"Where to?" she asks.

"Why am I the one who has to pick? You're the one who wanted to do this."

"Ugh, fine, be moody! Okay, I think I would like to start with the Statue of Liberty and Ellis Island."

We take a cab over to our destination while I try to remember why I thought this was a good idea. We get in line for the ferry where I buy our tickets, despite Peyton's overly dramatic argument as to why she should pay.

"So, tell me something about yourself," she asks while we are waiting in line.

I couldn't think of a more terrifying question to be asked. Nobody really wants to know about me. At least, not really. I hope I recover quickly enough to hide my look of dread. "What do you want to know?"

"The night at the club, you told me how you were in foster care. Tell me about that."

Well, she just went right for my weak spot. "What would you like to know?"

"I don't know. What age were you when you entered the system?"

"Ten," I answer, hoping she is satisfied with that.

"And do you mind me asking what happened that led to you going into foster care?"

"My parents were mugged and killed by a drunk driver. Neither of them had siblings and my grandparents on both sides were gone already."

She surprises me by looking up at me and grabbing my hand, giving it a squeeze. I'm used to people in the past looking at me with pity in their eyes, which I despise. They would stare at me as if I were damaged. All of that led to me discovering at an early age that it's easier to keep my past a secret. I'm not sure what made me blurt this out to Peyton, I usually deflect these questions. Perhaps I could sense that she would understand that a man like me is too proud to be looked at with pity.

"You made something of yourself despite those hardships in your life, good for you."

I don't know how to respond to that. Instead, I grab her hand and rush her to the top deck of the ferry. I've never seen the city from the Hudson River, but a part of me is kind of excited. Once we get situated in two seats in the corner of the upper deck, I sit back and unbutton the top few buttons of my dark blue, tailored dress shirt. Grabbing my aviator sunglasses, I lean back on the railing to get more comfortable.

"Look at you, Mr. GQ over here. You look like you should be on the cover of a fashion magazine." Peyton elbows me as she eyes me up and down.

"Are you saying you like what you see right now?" I wiggle my eyebrows, purposely trying to annoy her.

"Can you just take a compliment without insinuating anything?" I detect a hint of embarrassment because I believe she does, in fact, like what she sees. Little does she know; I feel the same about her.

"Are you deflecting my question, Peyton?"

"Oh, look at the view of the city," she ignores my question again. This time I allow it only to take in the view myself. It's a stunning sight to see the full view of the skyline. We both sit in comfortable silence as we take in the view. The distance from the city grows and the buildings begin to shrink in size.

We end up spending a couple hours on Ellis and Liberty Island, walking through the museums, and taking in the rich history. I find that Peyton and myself both enjoy understanding history, discovering why we are the way we are today. History is a great insight into the current times. I find myself laughing at Peyton's sense of humor and easy-going nature.

Once we make it back to Manhattan, we settle into our seats at a Michelin star restaurant. Peyton was saying how she had never been to a restaurant like this before, and I want her to experience it. The prices are high even for my standards, but I would like to do this for her.

"James, this is way too nice, we should go." Peyton begins to fidget in her seat.

"Nonsense, we are already seated."

"Good evening and welcome. Can I get you two something to drink to start your evening?" the waiter asks. Peyton looks at me incredulously and I can't help but suppress a chuckle at her shock.

"Yes, we will take a bottle of your 2017 Château Lafite Rothschild."

"Right away, sir."

"Come on, loosen up and enjoy the experience."

Peyton blows out a breath and nods her head. "You're right, I shouldn't waste this time being uncomfortable, but you are ordering my food for me."

I smile at that request. "Deal."

After the waiter pours us our glasses of wine, Peyton takes her first sip. "Wow! This taste's amazing! It's rich at first, but it softens."

"That's exactly right," the waiter interjects before he walks away.

I raise my eyebrow at her. "Look at you fitting in perfectly."

She shrugs her shoulders. "I love red wine, it's a passion of mine."

"Well, in that case, I'm glad I ordered this."

"Me too, thank you so much for this, James. It's too much, but I'm so appreciative."

My heartbeat picks up speed with the knowledge of pleasing her. With my ex, it was expected that we do fine dining and spend my money, all without any gratitude. Peyton is unlike most of the women I have surrounded myself with over the years. I try not to make any comparisons because I'll never want a relationship again, but she makes it hard to ignore these differences.

After we finish our meal, we are both tipsy from the bottle of wine, chuckling at each other like two teenagers. We walk down the street, arms linked, pointing out stores and restaurants along the way.

"You know, when you loosen up, you're not the man I expect you to be," she says, taking me by surprise.

"What man do you expect me to be?"

"I don't know, uptight. Someone who takes life too seriously, not willing to drop all responsibility and enjoy the moment."

We walk in silence for a moment as I mull over her words. Everything she is describing is *exactly* who I am, apart from when I am with her. She brings this side out of me, one that I thought died a long time ago.

"I normally am like that. I don't know what to say, you seem to bring it out in me."

She glances at me with a look of curiosity.

"What?" I ask with apprehension.

"It sounds like you are not too thrilled about that. Do you not like being around me? Would you prefer to not loosen up?"

I huff. "If I'm being honest...I don't know how I feel about it."

"That is honest." I hate that I see disappointment etched across her face.

We walk in silence the rest of the way to the hotel. I'm running through all the things that I should say to her, but none of them leave my lips. It seems too dangerous. I don't want to show too many of my cards. We continue to ride in silence up the elevator to our floor, where I walk her to her room.

"Look, I'm sorry about what I said. I know I'm a complicated person, but I really didn't mean anything bad by it."

"I know, I understand. For what it's worth, I like both sides of you, the serious one and the fun one. I think they're both worthy of being revealed."

Her words hit me right in the chest. No one has ever said something like that to me before. I look down at her and feel myself soften to her. For the first time in a long time, I long to be close to someone, to her. I long to feel her lips on mine, to caress her skin and run my hands through her hair. I can see it in her eyes that she wants me to kiss her, that she is feeling the same way that I am. I feel myself inch closer to her as her breaths quicken.

The elevator doors chime, breaking the trance that we were in. I clear my throat and take a step back, realizing what I almost did.

"Goodnight, Peyton. I will see you in the morning." I step back and move over to my room, right next door, grabbing my keycard and opening my door as quickly as possible.

Once I'm in the safety of my own room, away from her, I take a deep breath and lean against the door. Spending this much time with her is becoming dangerous. It feels like it's only a matter of time before I can't resist getting a taste of her lips.

I begin to undress and step into a warm shower, letting the heat of the water relax my tense muscles. When I close my eyes, I see Peyton's face looking at me with desire in her eyes. She licks her lips and slowly gets on her tippy toes as she leans in to press her lips to mine. My dick hardens as I imagine what it would feel like. Without thinking, I wrap my hand around my shaft and begin pumping up and down. I think about her deepening the kiss as her tongue plays with mine. My strokes become more aggressive just as our kiss done, when I imagine her moan into my mouth, I come instantly as hot bursts hit the shower floor.

The normal feel of satisfaction after a release is absent, re-placed with a stronger craving than before. I swipe my towel from the rack in anger at my inability to control these feelings. I wrap the towel around my waist and head into the room to get changed. As I'm digging through my suitcase, a gentle knock sounds at the joining door between our rooms. I look down at my towel and decide to ignore it until I can get some clothes on.

Just as I'm about to drop the towel, she knocks again, harder this time. I walk over to the door, already in a bad mood and swing the door open. She is standing there in pajama shorts and a t-shirt, makeup gone, hair in a ponytail, never having looked more beautiful. She opens her mouth to speak but must realize I'm in just my towel. Her mouth hangs open while her eyes are focused on my stomach. Her eyes look up and down, taking in everything. Why does she have to look at me like that? I'm already hanging on by a thread.

"I...I...," she stutters.

She can barely speak and knowing that I'm the reason does something to me. I take a couple steps towards her while her eyes bounce all over my body.

"Yes?" I whisper.

"I...," she continues.

"You?" my hand reaches up and caresses her cheek.

"I don't remember," she says, barely audible.

My other hand reaches up to her neck and we stand there, both breathing heavily. I can't help but look at her plump lips as the desire courses through me. My control has slipped, and I know I'm going to taste her. I'm just enjoying prolonging this moment between us, the agony of not having what is right in front you. She leans in closer, our lips now touching as we breath each other in. I catch her close her eyes as she waits, and my control finally snaps as our lips crash together. The kiss is controlled as our lips explore, alternating between soft and hard kisses.

I push her back against the wall and take control. My tongue finds her and the energy shifts from exploratory to hungry as our bodies meet. I push my hip against her as I grind myself on her. She lets out a small moan into my mouth where my control snaps and my desire for control takes over. I pull my head back and slowly caress my hand over her breasts before it reaches up to her neck. I'm about to put some pressure there before I realize who I'm with. It's like a bucket of ice is poured over me, and I step back quickly.

"What's wrong?" she says panting.

"I'm sorry, we shouldn't be doing this." I run a hand through my hair. "I almost...," I shake my head. I shouldn't say anything.

"You almost what?" she asks. "You almost squeezed my neck?"

"What?" I ask, alarmed.

"You almost squeezed, and I would have liked it. I was right there with you, James."

"No, I'm sorry. You deserve to be with someone who wants to be gentle and tender with you."

"Don't tell me what I deserve. I know what I want," she steps closer and puts her hand on my cheek.

"No," I whisper out as I remove her hand. "That never should have happened." I walk through the door and grab the handle. Before I close the door, I look at her one last time. "It's better this way."

Chapter Nine

Peyton

The ding of the airplane sound system breaks me from my trance. I glance around to see if anyone is looking at me. If they notice my discomfort. Everyone seems to be lost in their own world of electronics, including James. He hasn't been able to look me in the eyes all morning and afternoon. Our meeting with the vendor went well. They did a great job with their presentation and addressed all of our concerns with thoughtful solutions. In spite of all of this, my brain kept replaying the events of the day before.

I can't stop thinking about the feel of his lips on mine, how desperate I was for him to get rough with me. I could tell he wanted to and could sense the change in his demeanor. The way my bodied responded to his hand around my throat, I know I wanted it. I like knowing there is a rough of him in the bedroom. My body was begging for me to ask him to show me how he liked it. I'm not an innocent virgin by any means, but I have never been with someone who is dominant between the sheets. I didn't know I could possibly crave it until last night.

The only problem is that he seems to be ashamed of revealing this side of himself to me. After we stopped last night, I could see him put a wall back up between us. Which hurt me more than I would like to admit. Now he won't talk to me unless I initiate it. Even when he does respond, it's one or two words answers. When the flight ends, I book it to my Uber where I can finally take in a deep breath.

"Hi, dear. How are you doing?" my mom kisses my cheek as I plop myself down on the kitchen island stool.

I love the time I get to spend with my family. We have dinner together every Sunday, and it's always exactly what I need to recharge. The rest of the week was hell trying to work with James while he iced me out.

"I'm doing good. Can I help with anything?" I offer as I watch her chop vegetables.

"I think I have everything covered, you just relax and tell me about New York. Did you get a chance to explore?"

"I did. I saw the Statue of Liberty, Ellis Island, and I got to have dinner at a Michelin star restaurant."

"That sounds lovely. I imagine you did not have dinner alone," she says with a questioning tone.

"My boss, James, took me to dinner."

Before she can interrogate me any further my brothers charge through the door. Growing up with four brothers, I had to learn to be loud and tough to have my voice heard. The chaos that surrounds me is music to my ears.

"Dude, you smell like shit. How about you shower after you hit the gym?" Jackson shoves Logan.

"I save it just for you, asshole," Logan fires back.

"Boys! Can you at least wait until after dinner to act like animals?" my mom shouts in frustration.

We all gather around the island while mom continues to cook. Liam and Becca are the last ones to arrive, getting here just as we are taking our seats at the table.

"Sorry we're late," Liam says. "Becca wasn't feeling great, so I had her take a nap."

"I'm feeling much better now," Becca chimes in as she grabs a seat.

"You take all the naps you need, as long as you take care of that grandbaby of mine," dad says.

We make it through dinner with little bickering. You know the meal is a hit when everyone's too busy shoving their face. Jackson and I are stuck washing the dishes while everyone else retreats to the family room to relax.

"How's life at the hospital going?" I ask.

Jackson is a top cardiac surgeon in the city. Most people know him as someone who plays hard, but he works even harder. We are all extremely proud of him.

"Same as always, not enough hours in the day."

"Are you getting enough rest?" I begin putting the plates in the dishwasher after he rinses them.

"No, less than normal."

"You dating anyone right now?" He hands me the last dish that I put into the dishwasher before I close up.

"Nothing seriously at the moment," he smiles mischievously.

"I don't even want to know what is making you smile like that. Keep it to yourself, perv." I shove his shoulder as we walk into the family room to join everyone else.

"Greyson is being his typical elusive self." I catch Logan spout out as I find a seat next to Greyson on the couch.

"Leave him alone," I interject. "At least he knows how to keep some things to himself unlike someone else I know." I look right at Logan.

"There are plenty of things you don't know about, sis." Logan shakes his eyebrows at me.

"Son, women like a challenge. Maybe you would be settled down with a wife if you were a little more like Greyson," dad says.

"How about we all stop talking about me like I'm not in the room," Greyson speaks up. "And I'm not being elusive, I just don't want to give up personal details about my love life. Unlike you, I have some class."

"Good for you, sweetheart. Women deserve respect," mom smiles at Greyson while Logan rolls his eyes.

"Anyway, what's new in your life, sis?" Logan deflects.

"Oh, you never finished telling me about New York," mom says.

"You were in New York?" dad questions.

"Honestly, honey, do you ever pay attention when I tell you things?"

"I pay attention just fine. Why were you in New York?" dad deflects moms remark.

"For business. We were interviewing a potential vendor for our new ERP system."

I get everyone up to speed about why I was there and how everything went. After we discuss the success of the presentation, the guys start talking sports, leaving my mom and Becca to do their interrogations after I tell them about my night in the city.

"So, your boss, who is around your age, took you to a fancy restaurant and paid for your meal. While ordering an expensive bottle of wine?" she gazes at my mom, who is smirking right back at Becca.

"Why don't you two just spit it out already?" I huff out with frustration.

"Did anything happen between you two?" Becca whispers, while my mom looks at me curiously.

"Not exactly," I answer hesitantly.

"You're going to have to give us more information than that, dear!" mom says.

"Mom, dad is right there! I don't want to talk about this around him. And come to think of it, why would I tell *you* this?"

"Because I'm your mother and we're two mature adults who can talk about these things without acting like children."

"Ugh, fine," I eye Becca as if to place the blame on her for making me talk about this with my mom. She just shrugs like I need to get over it. "He walked me to my hotel room and things got heated. We ended up kissing and when things were about to go further, he froze. After that, he retreated and hasn't been able to make eye contact with me since."

"I bet he is torn. You're his employee, and he doesn't want to cross the line," Becca states like it is a fact.

"I agree," mom says. "He's just confused about his position in the company and how it would look."

"There's more to it than that. He has a dark past and has made it clear that he doesn't do relationships."

"Well, are you interested in him?" Becca asks.

The answer is sitting there, waiting to be released. For me to finally speak the truth that I have been desperately trying to ignore.

"Yes, I'm. I can't stop thinking about him." I say in a hushed tone, trying to keep the guys out of this conversation. "In the beginning, I just noticed his good looks. He was closed off and short with me and really new how to get on my nerves. Well, that part hasn't changed. But the longer I have been around him, the more I have seen sides of him that I really enjoy.

We have fun together and being around him is comfortable. But nothing could ever happen, like I said, he doesn't want a relationship."

"Men afraid of getting hurt always say that. You just need to make him see how much he wants you. I say you start making him jealous and start tempting him in the office," Becca chuckles at her idea.

"Oh, Becca you are so bad," mom laughs. "But I agree with her one hundred percent. I say you make sure he can't resist his attraction to you."

"And on that note, I'm heading home. I think I draw the line on my mom telling me to seduce a man."

Mom and Becca continue to laugh like they are teenagers. I roll my eyes and say my goodbyes to everybody.

On the way back into the city, I start to think about what they said. The idea *is* tempting, to seduce James and show him he can't resist what he wants. With him giving me the cold shoulder all week, maybe this is exactly what he deserves. I smile to myself thinking about what I can do come Monday morning to make him sweat.

Chapter Ten

James

I glance at the clock to see that it is ten minutes until Peyton is scheduled to meet me in my office. We put a deposit down with the company we met with in New York. They asked us to gather some data before they send out a team to put a game plan together. While I'm pleased with the progress that we have made, I'm not looking forward to seeing her. I haven't figured out how to act around her since the night in New York. I can't believe I lost control and kissed her. Not only is she relationship material, but she is also my employee. It could get messy if things went wrong, which they always do. The weekend did me some good to get some space. I'm hoping I can pull myself together and move forward professionally. Minutes later there is a light knock on the door.

"Come in," I shout from across the room.

Peyton walks in and my jaw drops. She looks like a freakin' wet dream as she struts towards me with a knowing smirk on her face. She is wearing a tight, black pencil skirt with a slit up the right leg, a red shirt tucked in, revealing the tops of her breasts, and red lipstick to match. When she gets to the table, she places her stuff down and leans against the table, breasts on full display. I do my best to avoid looking at her breasts but fail miserably.

"Good morning, boss." The authoritative name makes my hands clench in frustration.

"Morning, Peyton."

"How was your weekend?" She crosses her arms under her breasts, pushing them higher above her top. Today is going to be hell.

"Ugh, it was fine," I bite out and begin gathering my things to join her at the table.

"Mine was great! Thank you for asking," she smiles brightly at me like nothing ever happened between us. Like she isn't bothered in the slightest by my presence.

"Let's just get started," I grumble as I stand from my chair, meeting her at the conference table. She nods her head and starts settling in.

"I think we need to bring the department managers in again to help us gather the data that we need. I can draft an email to them laying out exactly what we need from each department."

"You can take the lead on that. I would like to have the final review of everything before it goes out the door."

"That isn't a problem. Let me take the lead and I will make sure you have the final review," she stands up and leans forward. "There is one thing I wanted you to look at. This graph shows the projection of how the cost will be incurred throughout the remainder of this year. I wanted you to have this in case the board has any questions."

I try to act interested in the numbers, but all I can do is stare directly down her shirt at the black lace bra that is pushing her breasts up. When my brain stops short-circuiting, I glance up at her and notice that smirk is back on her face. Is she doing this on purpose? I grab the paper out of her hand and scowl at her. I don't know what game she is playing, but she better be careful.

"Thank you, Ms. Brady. I think that is all we needed to discuss for today." Without another word I stand, walk back to my desk, and take a seat. Hoping she gets the message that she is dismissed.

I hear her let out a soft chuckle and head for the door after she gathers her things. I'm in some serious trouble if that is how she is going to act around me.

The day drags on, but I manage to get *some* work done, only thinking of Peyton every other minute.

The second Monday of every month I make a visit to my last set of foster parents, Ralph and Melinda. They were the only people in my life growing up that treated me like a person, and not like an inconvenience. They took me in when I was thirteen and I stayed there until I was eighteen. It was five years of the most love I had been surrounded by since my parents died. They continually ask me to come around more, but it must be out of pity. They know I have no one else. So, I have made it easy on both ends by doing a monthly visit.

I drive the ten minutes to their run-down house, which they refuse to let me pay to fix up, and park on the street. When I knock on the door, Melinda answers within seconds.

"How many times have I told you to let yourself in? You're family dear."

She is in her seventies and slowing down, but she does not let that get her down. I kiss her on the cheek before I walk through the door.

"You shouldn't leave the door open in the first place. I keep telling you this isn't the safest neighborhood."

"You worry too much. What could anyone take from us that has much value? We're simple people."

We begin walking to the back of the house, knowing exactly where Ralph is. Once we enter the family room, I hear the familiar sounds of the six o'clock news before I see him in his recliner, shaking his head at the journalist.

"It's a damn shame," he mutters.

"Ralph, turn that rubbish off and come say hello to Jameson," Melinda bellows.

"Son, you're here!" Every time he calls me that, my chest tightens.

"Nice to see you, Ralph." I shake his hand before he pulls me in for a hug. He always does this, and I'm always caught off guard by the affection.

"I have dinner warming in the oven. Let's go sit down so I can take it out." Melinda leads us to the small kitchen.

The place still holds memories of pleasant dinners shared around the table.

"So, Jameson, what's new in life?" Ralph asks once we take our seats.

"Work is still keeping me busy. We just hired a software company to help us implement a new system."

"Good to hear it. Anything else outside of work?" he pushes.

"Not really," I add.

"Oh, just ask him already," Melinda says. "Is there anyone special in your life?"

"No, I've told you two, I'm not looking for anything serious."

"Once upon a time, you were happily involved with someone special," Ralph states.

"And look how that worked out for me."

"I never liked Margaret," Melinda admits. "She was only after your money and status. Not everyone is like that."

"I understand that. I'm just not interested in trying to find someone who isn't that way. I'm much happier focusing on my work."

"I think you feel much safer focusing on your work, but that doesn't bring lasting joy into your life," Ralph tells me.

Melinda brings over her beef roast and potatoes that make my stomach growl, she always was the best cook.

"How about we enjoy this delicious meal instead of ruining it discussing my boring old life?" I say in an effort to get them off my back.

Melinda sighs as she puts the platter in the center of the table, taking her seat. "We just want to see you happy dear, and we know work cannot make you happy. But we will drop it... for now," she eyes me.

"How are you two doing?" I ask.

"We're doing great, as always. Ralph's blood pressure has been a little high these days. The doctor's say he needs to eat healthier and start working out."

"What do the doctors know?" Ralph mumbles.

I turn to him. "You better start taking care of yourself. You can't leave your wife alone, living in this old house and this kind of neighborhood."

"You have nothing to worry about. I'm not going anywhere," he takes before taking a swig of his beer.

"Maybe you should cool it on the beers for a while too," I suggest.

"That's what I told him," Melinda interjects.

"Oh, please. You two are delusional. I feel great, nothing to worry about."

Melinda and I look at him, unconvinced by his words. This conversation is not over, I will keep at him. I really do mean it, he can't leave Melinda here in this house all alone. I wouldn't be able to sleep at night knowing she was here all alone.

When the evening is over, I shake Ralph's hand and kiss Melinda on the cheek, thanking them for having me over. They walk me to the door, like they do every time.

"You know you don't need to thank us. We look forward to your visits. We just wish we could see more of you," Melinda says.

"I wouldn't want to take up too much of your time."

"Nonsense, son."

"I will see you two next month. Have a good evening."

They both exhale in unison at my deflection. I am sure they are used to it by now, but I don't want them to feel any obligation where I'm concerned. I am older now and can take care of myself.

On the drive home, I begin to think about what they said about my happiness. I enjoy my work, but maybe they have a point that it does not bring me true happiness. What does bring my joy right now? In that moment, Peyton comes to mind. I shake my head at the thought. That's highly inappropriate and a thought that I could never entertain, she deserves some-one who actually wants a real relationship, who can give her everything she has planned for her future. I know I fall short of what she wants. I fell short for Margaret, and I'm not even sure I can blame her.

Chapter Eleven

Peyton

"This is great work, Peyton," James says from his chair at his desk. I am sitting across from him at one of the seats opposite his.

"Thank you. I hope it's enough for them to get started."

"I'm sure it's more than they need. You clearly worked hard this week to gather this so quickly. I appreciate the commitment."

"I take my work seriously, and I know you're on a tight schedule." He skims through the spreadsheet one last time before he closes it out.

"I will send this over to Jim as soon as possible."

"Sounds good. Let me know if you need anything else in the meantime."

"Will do. Thanks again for the hard work." I nod at him with appreciation for the praise and absolute frustration at his formality.

He is getting on my last nerve. I know he's tempted, but he isn't making any sort of indication that he will budge and acknowledge our attraction. It's Friday, a whole week of flirtatious outfits and seductive looks. Of me leaning over his shoulder a little further than necessary, and him drooling like a fool. Now, I have given up on pride and am willing to push harder.

I stand from my chair and make my way to his side of the desk. Today I'm in a dark red dress that matches my lips with black stockings. He glares at me as I walk his way and lean against his desk.

"I have been meaning to thank you for that tour you gave me weeks ago at the club. It was very...informative. My friend, Janet, reminded me that tonight is the monthly *event*. I didn't want you to be thrown off if you saw me there, so I wanted to tell you now that I was going to go and...experiment." I had no intention of going, but he didn't need to know that. I adjust my legs to emphasize the slit in my dress. He takes notice and stares at my legs for a minute before he slowly skims up my body, his jaw clenched. I see the anger radiating off of him.

"Why the hell would you do that?" he barks out

"Why not? It looks fun, and I can't pretend that I'm not a *little* bit curious about what goes on behind those closed doors."

"You told me at the club you were just there for fun. Just to see what it was like, that's all."

"Well, I changed my mind. Now, I want to experience it."

"You couldn't handle it." He runs his hand through his hair.

"You don't know what I can handle."

He moves his hand to my thigh and squeezes, hard. I raise my eyebrows at his touch and hold my breath, hoping he continues. After what feels like an eternity, I see the moment the war waging in him comes to an end. I'm standing here waiting to see which side won when he uses his other hand to lift me up on his desk. My body is engulfed in flames at the realization that he has finally given in.

"How about I give you a little preview before you decide what you can handle?" he speaks into my ear as his hands come up to face.

I look up into his eyes and dare him with mine to make the first move. His lips come crashing down on mine as he takes complete control of this kiss. I'm just trying to keep up. I moan when I am greeted with his tongue against mine. My body is on fire like never before. When he breaks the kiss, he takes a couple steps back while keeping his eyes on my body.

"Get off my desk and stand by the window," he says as he takes a seat in his leather chair.

It takes my brain a minute to realize what he is asking of me. I get off the desk and walk on shaky legs to the window that's only a couple feet from his chair. When I turn to him, the desire in his eyes makes me feel slightly on edge.

"I remember that night in the club when I was showing you around. You were excited watching people have sex in front of everyone in the room. There are buildings surrounding us, people can easily look in here and see what we are doing. Does that excite you?"

I don't know how to answer that. Does it excite me? It's hard to tell through the nerves surging through my body at the moment, but I think I'm excited. I don't know how I feel about the realization that this turns me on.

"I'm not sure, maybe?"

"I think it does, Peyton. I think you like the attention. Now, take off that dress and show everybody what is underneath. You've been teasing me all week, and now that comes to an end."

I reach behind my back and slowly drag the zipper down my back, trying to work up the courage I need with each pull. Next, I push the straps of the dress off my shoulder one at a time. When I have the second one down, James moves his hands to his belt and begins unbuckling, followed by unzipping his pants. He reaches in and grabs his dick until it springs free out of his pants. I try to swallow but my mouth has seized to produce any moisture. With his dick in his hand, he begins stroking, giving me the courage to let my dress fall to the ground. Luckily, my seduction attempts this week have led me to wear a matching black bra and panties with my black thigh-high stockings.

"Fuuck," falls out of James' mouth in a whisper. "Take off your bra and play with your breasts for me."

It doesn't take long for me to do as I'm told. I begin massaging my breasts while watching him touch himself. All my nerves begin to fade away and I begin to feel bold. I reach into my panties and start to play along with him. He stands up, walks over to me, and grabs my hands placing them behind me as he backs me up against the window.

"I never told you to touch your pussy," he bites out with a bit of anger in his tone.

He takes his hands and begins massaging my breasts, letting his thumbs swipe over my nipples. While one hand stays on a breast, he leans his head down and starts sucking on the other nipple. At first it is gentle and sensual, but it doesn't take long before the sucks are hard and followed by bites. He eases the pain with a soft lick until he moves to the other breast to do the same. When he's finished with my breasts, he moves down to his knees, looking up at me with fire in his eyes before he slides my panties to the side.

"Are you going to let everyone watch me lick your pussy?"

My brain has lost the ability to articulate words, all I can do is vigorously shake my head up and down. I stand there watching, waiting for him to taste me. Instead of doing that, he just stares at my pussy before he takes his thumbs and spreads my lips. He brings one thumb over to swipe across my clit. My head falls back against the window, completely lost in this man worshipping me. When he takes his first taste, I decide I have to watch him, and the view does not disappoint. His eyes don't leave mine as his tongue expertly swirls around, making my legs begin to tremble. Eventually, he wraps a leg around his shoulder and doesn't hold back from completely devouring me. I'm on the brink of an orgasm when he inserts two large fingers into me and bends them. I go off like a rocket, and he moans into me once he feels my walls clenching all around.

I'm left standing here leaning against the window, trying to catch my breath. He stands up and wipes his mouth with the back of his hand before gently grabbing me and pulling me in for another kiss. Just as it's beginning to get heated again, he pulls away with force.

"Fuck... I don't have a condom."

He looks completely defeated by this realization. His fore-head falls to mine as he tries to calm his own breathing. I feel his arousal press up against my stomach. It only takes a second for me to decide to drop to my knees. He bites his lip as he watches me descend down his body until I'm face to face with his dick. I reach up and begin stroking with one hand before I bring my mouth to him and lick circles around the tip.

"Are you going to take all of me down, Peyton?" he says as he puts his hands on each side of my face.

I give him a slight nod of my head to give him permission to use me as he pleases. Heat grows in his eyes when he realizes what I just allowed of him. Without a moment of hesitation, he slams into my throat. At first, I struggle to take all of him, his length and thickness are much more than I'm used to. I can see him start to loss control. I try to create more suction to push him over the edge. In seconds, he is cursing as he spills down my throat. I have never been manhandled like that while going down on someone and I loved every minute of it.

We start to dress in silence as I try to think of the best way to handle this situation. Is he going to freak out and tell me this was all a mistake? The intercom buzzes as Angela's voice comes through.

"Mr. Davis, your meeting with Eric Weston is in ten minutes. Just wanted to give you a chance to prepare for his visit." James calmly walks over to the phone, leaving me to finish dressing myself.

"Thank you, Angela. Peyton and I are just finishing up." He finishes looping his belt while he walks to the door, pausing as he waits for me. "I'll see you Monday, Peyton."

That's all I get as he opens the door for me to leave.

Chapter Twelve

James

"Yes, I hear you loud and clear, sir." I slam the phone down, lean back in my chair, and try to collect myself.

The pressures of this job can feel overwhelming at times. Right now, the board is breathing down my throat. They want this project complete so they can move forward with an acquisition, the timeline given keeps shrinking. This is a nice distraction from the chaos I felt all weekend whenever I thought about Peyton. I've never enjoyed myself with a woman the way I did with her. I almost embarrassed myself and came the second her mouth touched me. Yet the problem still remains, I don't want a relationship and she is still my employee. My computer dings with an incoming email, pulling me out of my thoughts.

Good morning, Mr. Davis,

I just spoke with Jim on the phone. They will be coming to Chicago to meet with us on Tuesday of next week. I believe we have everything we need ready for the meeting. I will let Angela know so she can book the executive board room for the meeting.

Please let me know if there is anything else you would like me to prepare for this meeting.

Thank you,

Peyton

I'm disappointed that I cannot think of a reason for us to see each other until the meeting, which is eight days away. Come to think of it, I haven't been down to speak with Lance, her boss, since the start of the project. I should go down there to see how he is managing with Peyton's focus entirely on this project. I spin around in my chair and stand up, looking at the window that Peyton was leaning against the other day, knowing I'll never see that spot in the same light.

As I stroll out of the elevator, I adjust my tie and look down at myself, making sure I look put together. I'm not sure why I care what I look like all of a sudden. I make it down to the fifty-eight floor and my stomach flutters as I approach Peyton's office, willing myself not to peek inside. I lose that battle when I glance in her office to find her on the phone, talking animatedly while she throws her head back and laughs. Just when she peeks up and spots me, I stumble over myself, recovering before I completely lose my balance. The best idea I could come up with was to nod and keep walking. This is not me. I'm never this clumsy and out of sorts.

I head into Lance's office and tap on the door. He looks up from his computer, greeting me with a smile.

"James! To what do I owe the pleasure?"

"Just thought I would pay you a visit, see how everything is running in your department now that you're down a team member." I continue into his office and take a seat across from him.

"It's certainly busy! We put a large workload on Peyton, that much has become obvious. But the staff is up to the challenge, everyone is coming together to get the work done."

"I'm glad to hear it. Let me know if it becomes too much, I can see if there is any room to lighten her workload and give you some of her time."

"Will do, James, I appreciate that. Tell me, how is Peyton doing?" he asks with a curious gleam.

"Peyton is doing...," I stumble on my words, not wanting to give anything away about my feelings, yet wanting to be honest about her performance. "...exceptional. She's a very head strong, intelligent woman and has a great work ethic. Thank you for recommending her."

"I knew she would impress you. She's the best of the best, and I see how hard she has been working on this project, putting in overtime every night." I had no idea she was staying late every night, it's usually just me putting in those hours.

"I had no idea she was working late so often. I wish I could say it was going to slow down soon, but once we meet with DRN next week, we're going to be moving quickly."

"I'm sure she understands that. Maybe I'll take her out for dinner tonight to celebrate her successes. It'll also get her out of the office on time for once."

"Lovely idea, Lance. I think I'll join you two to celebrate."

"Oh, uh, yes, that would be fantastic. I'll let Peyton know; I am sure she will be happy to have the CEO attend."

I nod my head instead of saying anything to cause suspicion to my sudden interest in joining them for dinner.

"Just let me know the time and place." I stand and walk out of the office, passing Peyton once again who smiles at me as I walk by. What am I doing? This feels like dangerous territory for me.

A couple hours later, I get an email from Lance letting me know that Peyton has agreed and to meet them at a nice Italian restaurant at five-thirty. I agree and get back to work for the rest of the day, for once, excited to leave work on time.

At five o'clock, I shut my computer down and head to the bathroom in my office to freshen up. I get to the restaurant early and text Lance to let him know I have gotten our table. He lets me know they are five minutes away, which gives me time to look over the wine list and select a bottle of red that

I think Peyton will enjoy. They approach the table just as the waitress has opened the bottle of wine.

"Good evening, Peyton." I stand to pull out her seat, sitting her to my left.

"Evening, James. Thank you," she says as she takes a seat.

Lance sits across from me. "Good evening, boss."

"Lance," I nod. "I hope it is alright that I already ordered the wine. It's a classic red blend that I thought we could enjoy."

Peyton takes a sip. "Mmm, it's delicious."

"I'm glad you like it." I smile as I watch her lick her lips as she enjoys the wine.

"So, Peyton, James has updated me on how well you're doing. We wanted to take you out to dinner to celebrate your successes and say thank you for your hard work."

"Wow, I don't know what to say. Thank you, I appreciate the opportunity to take this project on."

"You were the right one for the job," I add.

I notice the slight embarrassment she is feeling at these compliments and cannot help but think how adorable she looks. Suddenly, I wish we were alone.

A half hour has past, and we have ordered and just received our food. We have finished the bottle of wine, loosening up enough to enjoy the evening more freely. Lance is telling a story about Peyton's first week at the company, where she got stuck working with a previous employee who tested her patience one too many times. She ended up calling him out in a department meeting in front of everyone, embarrassing him but effectively ending his misogynistic remarks.

"I knew she would be a force to be reckoned with after that," Lance laughs.

Peyton smiles. "He was the worst; I couldn't hold back. I was so embarrassed afterwards. Like you said, it was my first week.

Part of me wished I could have held it together without losing my cool."

Lance waves his hand. "He had it coming, he picked the wrong woman to mess with."

I smile at the thought of Peyton putting someone in their place on her first week. Her confidence in herself and her talent is extremely attractive. I find myself staring at her while she is talking to Lance, noticing her full lips, and remembering what they taste like. Thinking about what other parts of her taste like makes my dick begin to grow. I readjust myself under the table, but my brain keeps taking me back to that day in my office.

"Excuse me, I'm going to use the restroom." I stand up, hoping no one notices my predicament, and walk in the direction of the restroom.

After I use the restroom and wash my hands, I stand at the sink for a moment longer trying to recover. Once I feel like I have control, I open the door and run into someone.

"Oh, gosh, sorry!" Peyton says. "I was just on my way to use the restroom as well."

We're still standing inches from each other, but I can't seem to put space between us. She smells incredible, a mixture of sweet and sultry. The scent seeps in and clouds my brain making my body lean in for more.

"Thank you for taking me out tonight," she whispers.

"It's my... pleasure," I say as I look her up and down. Her body seems to shudder at my words.

"Well, I should hurry and use the restroom." She makes no move away from me.

"Okay." We both stand where we are, breathing heavy.

"James," she sighs in a barely audible voice.

"Peyton?" I return with no more self-control than she seems to have at the moment.

"Please...," I don't let her finish before my lips are on hers.

She moans in response as she opens her mouth for me in an instant. I grab her face and deepen the kiss, incapable of slowing this down. She runs her hands up my back and through my hair before she presses her body into mine. I growl at the friction and step her back against the wall where I can press my hips into her. Grabbing her leg, I'm ready to wrap it around me, when we hear chatter as two women approach the hallway. I drop my hands and back away from her, watching her chest rise up and down, wishing we were alone for me to kiss my way along her breasts.

"We should get back to Lance," I say. She nods her head in agreement and fixes her hair and dress as I do the same. "I'll go first, you go ahead and use the restroom."

When I get back to the table and take a seat, Lance raises his eyebrows and smiles.

"Sorry about that, I ran into an old friend," I lie.

"No worries. Thank you for joining us tonight, I'm sure it means a lot to Peyton to receive the recognition."

"I'm happy to show my employees my appreciation."

A moment later, Peyton joins us back at the table. Her lips look slightly swollen from our kiss, making it impossible to take my eyes off of them. Wasn't that the exact reason I had to excuse myself to the bathroom, because I got lost in her lips? Luckily, the waiter comes and delivers our check, giving me a distraction as I pull out my card. Once the bill is taken care of, we stand and walk to the front of the restaurant.

"Peyton, thank you again for your hard work. I will see you two tomorrow at the office." Lance waves and walks out the door, leaving the two of us behind.

"How are you getting home, can I offer you a ride?" I suggest.

"Oh, I actually drove to work this morning. I wasn't sure if I was going to leave the city after work to visit a friend. I parked right next door in the small parking lot."

"Let me walk you to your car."

"Okay, thank you."

We leave the restaurant and begin walking to the parking lot next door. It's small and surrounded by brick walls. The night air has a bit of a chill to it, indicating the change from summer to fall is approaching. I watch Peyton walk next to me from the corner of my eye, craving her kiss. My body is on fire when she is near. When we reach a black BMW, she stops and turns to face me.

"This is my car. Thanks again for everything, James."

"No problem." I slowly close in on her. "I'll see you tomorrow, Peyton."

She looks up at me and time seems to stand still. I can see her waiting for me to make a move, and I try to hide the smile beginning to take root. I was just going to kiss her on the cheek, now I have other ideas.

Chapter Thirteen

Peyton

He is looking at me like he knows what I want, like it amuses him to see me squirm, and it's pissing me off. I start to turn towards my door to get in, but he grabs my arm to stop me and spins me around.

"Where do you think you're going?" he demands.

"Well, I don't feel like standing here all night staring at each other, so I'm going home." I make a second attempt at opening my door when James turns me around again.

"You're cute when you're flustered." His stupid smirk has turned into a full-on grin.

"What makes you think I'm flustered?" I fold my arms under my chest.

He steps into my space until I'm completely backed up against the car. "Tell me what you want, Peyton."

"What are you talking about?" I whisper on an exhale.

My entire body feels like an inferno with him this close to me. What I want is for him to kiss me, to make me come again.

"If you tell me, I may give it to you." He slowly runs his hand up and down my arm and I gulp down the saliva building in my mouth. My body is *begging* me to tell him.

"I...I want...you to kiss me... to...make me come again." I look up to see desire in his eyes. He looks like he wants to attack me but is trying to hold himself back. He closes his eyes and takes a deep breathe. "James...," I begin to say but he cuts me off.

"Peyton, there are so many things I want to do to you right now. I'm just not sure if you want them to." If my panties were not soaked before, they are now. I want him to do everything to me, I don't care what it is, if I have done it before or not. I trust him completely.

"Do them, all of them. Please...," I beg.

That was all he needed. He grabs me by the back of my neck and slams his mouth to mine. This kiss is too intense to be clean, we have skipped past the slow start and went straight for tongue and hot pressure. He abruptly breaks the kiss and backs away from me.

"Walk over to the front of your car and put your hands on the hood, now."

I recognize the switch from passion to anger. The fire in his eyes tells me to do as I'm told. I take shaky steps around my car until I reach the front. I look over at him as I bend slowly and place both hands on the hood. We stare at each other, me waiting for his next command. He begins taking slow and calculated steps towards me until he is standing directly behind me. My nerves are on high alert, anticipating what his next move is going to be, but my body is also craving his attention.

"You've been tempting me with this body for weeks." He brings his fingers to the back of my neck and begins trailing them down my spine. "Do you know what happens to women who tempt me?" His fingers graze over my bottom until they hook under my dress and flip it up, revealing my red, lace panties. I'm so captivated by where his hand is, I forget to answer his question. He grabs my hair with a fist and yanks my head back. I cry out in pain while a fresh wave of pleasure runs through my body. "Answer me when I talk to you."

"Ahh, no! What happens to women who tempt you?"

He leans down and whispers in my ear. "They get punished. Do you think I should punish you?"

"I don't know," I say, which is all I can come up with.

"I think you need to learn your lesson."

He pulls my hair to the side, exposing my neck and begins trailing his lips along the way. When he reaches my shoulders, he gives it a kiss before I feel the loss of his body on mine. In an instant, I feel the slap of his hand on my bottom cheek. The pain radiates through my body, all the way to my core.

"That was for all those sexy outfits you've been wearing around me, tempting me with your perky breasts and tight ass." He winds up and slaps my other cheek and I gasp out as my head falls forward on the hood. "That was for making me crave you the way I have. I can't get you out of my mind and it's driving me crazy."

My heartbeat accelerates at his admission. I'm glad I am not the only one feeling that way. Feeling out of sorts and stir crazy with these pent-up emotions. I have a feeling that all of our interactions were like foreplay, leading up to this explosive moment. He gives one final blow to my ass, leaving his hand there as he rubs soothing circles as to offer support for the pain.

"That was so you think of me tomorrow whenever you sit down." He squats down and begins pulling off my panties. "Now that we have taken care of that, I need another taste of this pussy."

He spreads my cheeks and licks his way from my clit up to my ass where he draws circles with his tongue. My brain is trying to catch up with the one-eighty from pain to pleasure. My body seems to know what it wants as I get on my tippy toes, trying to give him better access. He takes that invitation and goes back to my clit to lick and suck like a man starved. I feel my orgasm building as he begins to flick his tongue up and down, back and forth.

"Oh, fuck. Keep doing that, keep doing that... I'm gonna come," I moan out.

"Yes," he says in between flicks. "Come all over my face. Let me taste you."

His words send me over the edge as my orgasm hits with fury. The explosion courses through my body, more powerful than any orgasm I have ever had. I try to keep my moans down, but I know I'm doing a horrible job. My body goes limp as I rest on the hood of the car, trying to take in what just happened. I turn around and see James unbuckle his belt and lower down his pants. When he pulls his cock out, my body ignites all over again. This man can turn me on like no one ever has. He begins stroking himself as I bite my lip, watching in awe. He reaches into his pocket and pulls out a condom, sheathing himself as he slowly strokes down his cock.

"Please," I beg with frustration. "I need to feel you inside of me."

"Are you desperate for my dick?" he asks.

"Yes!" My hips begin to move back and forth, impatient for him.

I see him look up in the distance and a small smirk begins to form, he looks back at me.

"Looks like we have an audience. I know you like to be watched, Peyton. Let's give them something to look at."

With that, he moves his cock to my entrance and thrusts inside. My hands slam on the hood, trying to hold onto anything that will anchor me. I look up and see a man standing by his car, watching us. I should be freaking out, telling James to stop, but my body loves it. I feel my pussy clench around James as my arousal builds.

"You like that, don't you? Someone standing there, watching you get fucked on the hood of your car like a slut?"

He grabs my hips and begins slamming into me. I have never felt more filled before; his size is impressive. His thrusts are reaching areas that have never been touched.

"Fuck, you look so sexy taking me like this," he says as he picks up speed. "I'm gonna come so hard."

I close my eyes so I can concentrate on the sensations. My second orgasm builds as my walls begin to squeeze around him. He groans as he feels me clenching him and begins to lose his rhythm. I feel his climax hit him, then we both come down on top of the car, trying to catch our breath as we lay there, the sounds of the city all around us. I glance up and see the man get in his car and begin to back out. James eventually pulls out of me and stands up, taking off the condom and tossing it in the trash a few feet away.

I stand up and put myself together as James comes back towards me. This version of James is tender as he gently takes my face in his hands and kisses me.

"That was quite an end to the evening," he grins at me.

I laugh. "You can say that again."

"I think I'm going to need a repeat. I didn't get to worship this body of yours," he says as he runs his hands up and down my frame.

"Oh yeah? And I didn't get to taste you again."

He groans. "Fuck, you're making me hard."

"You recover quickly." As much as I would like another round, I know I should slow this thing down. I don't even know what we are doing. "Well, I should get going, it's getting late."

He nods his head and places a kiss to my forehead. "I'll see you at the office tomorrow."

"Goodnight, James."

Chapter Fourteen

Peyton

I walk into the office in the morning with a skip in my step. Although sleep didn't come easily, as I kept replaying the evening, I feel like I'm on top of the world. No man has ever been able to do to my body what James did. It was liberating to completely give up control, not having to worry about what I should do next or what he wants from me. I was just there to enjoy and let him take what he wanted. Although, it felt like all I did was receive.

"Morning, Peyton," Lance stops by my office, coffee in hand.

"Morning, Lance. Thank you again for last night," I say as I fire up my computer.

"Not a problem, I'm glad you enjoyed yourself. I'll let you get to it."

I spend the morning catching up on emails and trying to get some of my normal job duties finished. With the project at a standstill until we have our meeting next week, I have some time to get back to my normal role, not that it'll last very long.

I get lost in my work when I hear a tap on the door. When I look up, I see James watching me with a grin on his face.

"What's so funny?" I ask.

"Nothing, you just look really cute when you're concentrating so hard."

He walks further into my office until he reaches the side of my desk and sits. I wasn't ready for such a charming statement to fall from his lips, it throws me off a bit. We are just having sex, I remind myself, right? He told me he is not capable of more, but right now he is not acting that way.

"To what do I owe the honor of your presence?" I ask.

"I was wondering if you wanted to go out to lunch."

"Yeah, sure." I lock my computer and grab my purse. "Where too?"

Why does this feel so normal? Him asking me out to lunch is anything but normal. Yet, we begin walking comfortably next to each other until we arrive at a bistro down the block. Before we stop to walk inside, he pulls me into him and kisses me.

"I've been wanting to do that since I walked into your office." He gently places his lips back on mine.

All I can do is smile at him because I'm at a loss for words. He takes my hand and leads me into the restaurant, finding a booth near the back. We place our orders after discussing what we think they do best here.

"What do you think about coming over tonight?" he whispers, leaning over the table.

I laugh at his sudden playful behavior and whisper back. "I think I would enjoy that. Are there going to be orgasms?"

He chuckles. "There will be as many orgasms as you would like."

"Then text me the time and place. I'll be there."

Our food comes and we fall into easy conversation. We eat quickly in order to get back to the office, both having a lot of work to get done if we're going to leave on time to see each other tonight. When we get back to the building, before we enter, he pulls me aside and kisses me so slowly my body feels like it will melt into a puddle. He breaks the kiss, rubbing his thumbs over my cheeks.

"That should last me until tonight," he says.

The day seems to creep along, minutes passing by like hours. Finally, five o 'clock hits, and I shut down my computer. James had texted me earlier to give me his address and tell me to come over around seven. That gives me just enough time to get home, take a shower, and get ready before I have to leave for his place.

I opt on taking the L back to my place, to save on time. I shower and get ready in just over an hour, spending extra time shaving and putting on lotion. When I take a final look in the mirror and approve of my appearance, I head out of my apartment and decide to walk the fifteen minutes to his place. I'm in comfortable flip-flops and could use the time to myself.

I knock on his door, the top floor of an expensive apartment building, nerves dancing around at the realization that I am at my boss's place. Before I have time to really get in my head, he answers the door wearing a white t-shirt and jeans. Why do men always look so hot dressed like this?

"Hey." He meets me with a smile and a glass of red wine as I walk through the door.

"Wow, I could get used to this kind of treatment. Thank you!" I say as I take the glass from him.

"Come... let's go sit down."

Leading me to the couch of his apartment, I can't help but take in the view of the Chicago River from his panoramic view. The lights glisten off the river displaying the reflection of the skyline.

"Well, you definitely have an incredible view here," I say.

"Thanks, it's my favorite part about this place."

"I can see why." We sit and he scoots closer to me, giving me a quick kiss on the lips.

"Thanks for coming over tonight."

Why he is being so sweet? Does he even realize he is doing this? It is messing with my head, making me confused.

"Thanks for having me."

We fall into easy conversation, like usual, teasing each other and laughing at each other's jokes.

"You're a witty one, you know that?" he says.

"I had to be, growing up with four brothers."

"I keep forgetting about that. What's it like to have a big family?"

"Fun at times, annoying as hell at others. My family is my rock but sometimes they treat me like I can't handle myself."

"Oh, come on! If any woman can, it's you."

"Care to share that with them?"

"Absolutely! Just give them my number. I'll tell them all about your strengths, and how good you are at seducing me."

you are the one who has initiated each time, so enough with this seduction crap. You don't have to come on to me, I'm not forcing that on you." I fold my arms across my chest in an act of annoyance.

He throws his head back and unashamedly laughs, my favorite laugh of his, when he is completely in the moment and himself. "I know you're not forcing me princess, but I like the sound of that. Care to give it a try?" he wiggles his eyebrows at me.

I press my legs together in an effort to calm my body down. His words seem to have a way with me, they ignite something in me that has never been provoked before. He seems to notice the movement and squeezes his lips together, looking like he is angry at my reaction to his words.

"You would like that, wouldn't you?" I tease, trying to make light of the current situation.

"No, I would like to force you. Make you beg for me to stop, while I lick you up." He inches closer to me. I am panting at this point, and he knows it.

He smirks at me. "Does that turn you on? Thinking about me pinning you down while I take what I want?"

"Maybe," I say breathlessly.

He lifts his hand to my face and tucks my hair behind my ear. "I'm going to give you a five second head start to my bedroom over there." He points in the direction of his room. "Then I'm going to come after you, and I want you to struggle. Do you understand me, Peyton?"

I nod my head, being rendered speechless. My panties are wet, and my heart has accelerated so intensely, I feel the thundering of it on my chest.

"Good," he leans in and whispers in my ear. "Ready, set...go."

I take off as fast as I can, momentarily lost, trying to recall where he pointed. He's already at three when I am just at his bedroom door. I run in and shuffle as I try to figure out where to go. Once I decide on the bathroom, I'm running again as my heart pounds in my chest. Just when I approach the bathroom door, I feel his arm wrap around my waist and draw me into him.

"Got you!" he barks in my ear.

I struggle to get free, twisting and turning my body.

"That's right, you're stuck," he growls. "But I admire the effort." He whips me around and grabs my jaw with force. "Now, get on your knees."

Slowly, I drop to my knees. I want to shout *hell yes* because I have been craving his taste. When I look back up at him for guidance, he breaks character for a second and smiles kindly at me. It only lasts a second before he catches himself and his grimace is back.

"Now take out my cock and suck it."

I follow his command and unzip his pants with shaky hands as they pull out his impressive cock. Giving it a couple strokes, I open my mouth and swirl my tongue around the tip. Once I take him to the back of my throat, he throws his head back and groans. This time is different, he is letting me call the shots. I alternate between hard and sloppy sucks to gentle and teasing. He eventually breaks my suction, pulls me up to my feet, and slams his lips to mine.

"Fuck, you're good at that, but it's my turn now. Take off your clothes and get on my bed."

I want to have a little fun with him, so I opt to take off running towards the door. His reaction time is quick, he is on me within seconds, wrapping both his arms around me.

"Nice try but you can never escape me. If I want you," he spins me around. "I will have you."

Backing me up onto the bed, he pins my arms above my head with one hand. He uses the other hand to unbutton my jeans and work them off of my legs.

"I was going to taste you, but now I'm just going to fuck you."

"I don't want it," I say in my best fearful voice. "Please, stop."

"Well, that's too bad. Now get on your hands and knees, before I make you."

When I am on my knees, he pulls down his pants, puts on a condom, and slides into me. Grabbing my hips, he begins pumping in and out with expert precision, knowing exactly where to hit. We're both lost in the moment, moaning, and screaming when he flips me over on my back and slides back in. We're face to face for the first time while he is inside of me, looking into each other's eyes. It feels more intense this way. He slows his pace down and his slack jaw gives away his satisfaction. I feel my orgasm build, but I try to hold it off. I want to enjoy this moment, but it takes over as I scratch my hands down his back, trying to ground myself to something. My walls pulse around him which sets his own release off.

"Fuuuck," I drawl out, repeating myself several times.

He laughs. "Yeah," he breathes out. "Fuck is right."

We both begin to giggle after my little outburst at the end, and before you know it, we are in a fit of laughter, the kind you can't stop. I have never had such an intense orgasm followed by such hilarity. Just when I think I'm done, I think over at him and see him smirking, and lose control again.

"Okay, I think if you laugh anymore right after I give you an orgasm, I'm going to begin to get self-conscious," he says.

"I'm sorry," I wipe a tear running down my eye. "I don't know what came over me. I think I was a bit over dramatic at the end."

He smiles. "I like you being overdramatic."

Eventually, we collect ourselves and he pulls out to go clean himself up. When he returns, he dresses and sits on the edge of the bed. Something must have happened while in the bathroom because he looks uncomfortable.

"I don't do sleepovers, Peyton."

Where did that come from? We literally *just* finished. Was I supposed to be gone by the time he got back? I don't understand this change in demeanor. We were just having fun. How could I have led him to think I was trying to get cozy and overstay my welcome?

"I never said you did," I huff out, gathering my clothes and getting dressed.

"Look, no need to get angry with me. I just wanted to make sure you knew that. To make sure you know where we stand."

"I think you made it clear *exactly* where we stand." I storm out of the bedroom to the front door where I start to get my shoes on. He follows me out, standing there with his hands in pockets looking nervous.

"Peyton don't be like this. I didn't mean it like that. You don't have to high tail it out of here."

I laugh. "I think I do. I hadn't even completely recovered from what we just did before you flipped a switch and were practically pushing me out the door. Maybe you should just start paying me because that is how you just treated me, like a whore."

He runs his hands through his hair. "Look...I'm sorry. I never meant to make you feel like that. I haven't had a woman over here in years, I panicked. I didn't want you to get the wrong idea about what we are."

"And what are we?" I fold my arms across my chest like I do when I'm frustrated.

"I...I don't know. It's complicated. We're friends, and we have fun together. We enjoy each other sexually," he grunts. "This is why I go to the club. Sex complicates things, and I don't want to lead anyone on. I don't want to hurt you and I can't be the man you need. I can't offer you everything you deserve."

Chapter Fifteen

James

I hate this. I hate seeing her hurt face, the way she flinched when I spoke those words. I wish she understood that I could never be the one for her. I could never be the one for anyone. This is about protecting her, not about protecting myself, but she doesn't get it.

"I don't know what it is you think that you can't offer me, but I never asked for anything. I have never given you any reason to believe I have many expectations from you, outside of not being treated like a throw away rag."

Fuck, she's right, I know she is. I shouldn't have kicked her out before she was even dressed. It was a dick move. I just needed her to know where we stand, a conversation that should have happened before we started fooling around.

"I know, you haven't done anything wrong, it's me. I overreacted and treated you poorly when I should have just had an honest conversation. Look, I'm not going to lie, I care about you. I wouldn't be breaking all my rules if I didn't. But I just need you to understand that it still doesn't change what I want, but I *am* sorry."

She shakes her head and sighs. "It's okay, I may have overreacted at your comment too. I believe that you weren't trying to kick me out right away. It was just poor timing on your part to bring it up. And as much as I don't understand what is happening between us, I do know that I don't want it to end."

The truth is, I don't want it to end either. But is it fair to her to keep doing this when it can't go anywhere? Can I even stay away from her if I wanted to? Probably not, I'm not that good of a guy, clearly.

"I don't want it to end either." I step towards her and gently pull her into my arms. "I just don't want you to get hurt in the end. Can you just tell me if it gets too confusing for you, so we can end it before you hate me?"

She giggles. "I hate you half the time already, so I think I can manage that request."

I laugh at her response. It's a relief to be able to have this level of honesty with each other. Maybe we *can* do this without anyone getting hurt.

"Thank you for forgiving me. You don't have to leave right now."

"No, I should. It's getting late and we have to work tomorrow."

Although part of me wants her to stay a while longer, we say our goodbyes and she's out the door. While I'm taking a shower, I realize how nice it was having her here. It can get lonely in this big place all by myself. She filled it with something it has been missing for years, laughter.

Two weeks have flown by. We met with DRN and settled on an agreeable timeline. They have already sent us three consultants that are occupying a meeting room for the foreseeable future. It's been constant meetings with consultants and department heads. Peyton has been a huge help as always. We have gotten into a good rhythm with our after-work routine. Alternating our time between each other's place. We're having fun and enjoying our time together. We established a no sleepover rule, so no one gets confused.

Today has been a particularly hard day. I have had managers approaching me with requests for the new system and what they would like to see change. The board is breathing down my throat, and I haven't seen Peyton outside of work in three days. I fire off a text to her before the day is over asking her to come to my place tonight. I even offered to have dinner ready for us, which is a first. I breathe a sigh of relief when she texts me that she will be there, which is exactly what I need to help alleviate this stress.

Once I'm home, I order takeout from a local Italian restaurant and take a shower to wash the day off of me. The food arrives shortly after I get out of the shower, which I store in the oven to keep warm. I find my best bottle of Cabernet, Peyton's favorite, and open it up just as she knocks on the door. When I open it and see her standing there in cut off jean shorts and a tank top, I can't help but take her by the hips and smash my mouth onto hers. I deepen the kiss and suddenly we're a mixture of battling tongues and hands grabbing at each other. When I release my grip on her and we reluctantly pull away from each other, we're panting and out of breath from the intensity of the moment.

"Mmm, I like that greeting," she says in a raspy voice.

"Sorry, I can't be held accountable for my actions when you wear those shorts."

We get caught up in the evening, eating and drinking, when she gets a text message.

"Oh my gosh!" she stands up excitedly.

"What?" I jump up, thinking something is wrong. "Is everything okay?"

"Yes! My sister-in-law is in labor! I'm going to be an aunt!!"

At first, I feel relief that nothing is wrong which only lasts for a second before the familiar stabbing pain that accompanies these moments floods in.

"Congratulations, that's amazing!" I say, hoping my excitement is believable because I'm, of course, happy for her.

She jumps into my arms and squeezes her arms around my neck. I wrap my arms around her, shocked at how much her touch can calm any storm inside me.

"I can't believe it," she whispers. "I have to call my mom."

She walks out of the family room and into my bedroom to make her phone call. When she comes back, she is smiling ear to ear.

"Well, the baby is coming fast. She just got to the hospital an hour ago and she's already pushing."

"Are you going to go to the hospital?"

"No, I will give the parents and grandparents their time with the baby. I'll go tomorrow, maybe leave work a bit early."

"Now, what do you think your boss would think of that?" I joke as she takes a seat next to me on the couch.

"I don't know. I suppose I could persuade him tonight. I have a couple ideas in mind." She smiles at me mischievously.

"Let's see what you got, woman!" I say as I lay back on the couch.

Her head falls back as she laughs at my theatrics. She looks at me with fire in her eyes before she climbs on top of me, "Let the show begin, *Mr.* Davis."

Greg walks into my office bright and early the next morning. He's tried to get me to go out with him over the last month, despite dodging his calls. It's easier to ignore him than to have to explain why I have no interest in going to the bars or club with him. I don't even understand it myself.

"Dude, what the hell? Did I do something to piss you off that I don't know about?"

I laugh at his dramatics. "No, you didn't do anything. I've been...busy."

"Busy. Too busy to go out at midnight? I know you work hard, but not that hard."

"I never said I was busy with work."

"Why are you being so vague? What is keeping you so busy?" He leans forward on his chair, resting his forearms on his knees, like my answer is going to be something extreme.

"Chill out, you're being ridiculous. It's really not a big deal, I've just been hanging out with someone."

"You've just been *hanging* out with someone. I'm guessing this *someone* is a woman, or you wouldn't be so weird about it."

"So, what if it's a woman?"

"Who is it?" he asks with a smile on his face.

"It doesn't matter. We're just having fun. It's not anything serious. She knows that and is cool with it."

He begins *laughing* in my face. I crumble a piece of paper in front of me and chuck it at him.

"What the hell is so funny?" I demand.

"The fact that you think you can repeatedly have sex with a woman and have her stay *cool* with it. *And* the fact that *you* think you don't already have feelings for her. She must be special for you to break your rules."

"Think what you want. We're both having fun and keeping it casual. There are no feelings involved."

"It's that IT chick from the club, isn't it?"

I'm not in the mood for him to make any inappropriate comments about Peyton. His knowing cocky grin appears stuck on his face.

"What makes you say that?"

"Just a feeling," he shrugs.

"It doesn't matter who it is, because it isn't going to go anywhere."

"Whatever you say."

I decide we just need a subject change; this current topic is making me uncomfortable. I don't have feelings for Peyton. I mean other than enjoying her company and the sex, there are no deeper emotions.

"Enough about me. Anything new going on in your life? I *am* sorry I've been dodging your calls. I figured you would react like...well, just like you are reacting now."

"It's cool man, I'm just messing with you. But if I can give my two cents, it wouldn't be the worst thing in the world if you did have feelings for her. I would hate to lose a wingman, but you deserve to be happy. Anyway, I'm doing good, work is starting to ease up."

We spend the next twenty minutes talking and joking around. When I look at the clock, I realize I need to get some work done before my ten o'clock meeting. I tell Greg that I will call him soon so we can hang out, maybe go golfing or out for drinks. He reminded me that our friendship was not based on getting girls together and that we can just hang out, making me feel like an asshole for avoiding him.

After lunch I'm sitting at my desk, wondering whether Peyton has left for the hospital yet. After another hour of not being able to get my work done thinking about her, I decide to text her.

Me: You leave for the hospital yet?

Fifteen minutes later, a long fifteen minutes, I hear the alert that I received a message. When I open it, I smile at the picture of Peyton taking a selfie.

Peyton: I'm an auntie to a beautiful girl!

Me: She's beautiful. Congratulations! You are beautiful too!

The brief interaction was enough for me to put my head down and focus on work. Around five I begin to get antsy again, wanting to reach out to her. Instead, I decide to call it quits for the night and head home. When I get back to my apartment, I order dinner and kick back with a glass of bourbon and ESPN. It feels nice to get off work on time and have enough time to watch sports and have a drink.

A little while later, my phone rings. I reach for it in my pocket and see Peyton's name on the screen.

"Hello?"

"Hey you. How's it going?"

"Not bad. Just watching some tv and having a drink."

"It's only six. I'm surprised you aren't still at work."

"Yeah, I couldn't focus so I figured I would call it quits. What are you up to?"

"Just leaving my parents place, heading home."

"Wanna head here instead?"

She pauses for a minute. I'm about to tell her she does not need to when she speaks. "Yeah, I can do that. As long as you don't mind the fact that I'm gross right now. I've spent the day in a hospital and running around town with my mother."

"I think I can handle it. Come over." Do I sound too eager?

"Okay. I'll be there in about thirty minutes. I expect to be served my usual glass of wine when I walk through the door."

I laugh. "Yes, ma'am. See you soon."

We hang up and I sit back on the couch, relaxed and happy for the first time in a long time.

Chapter Sixteen

Peyton

When I show up at his apartment, he is standing there in his boxer briefs holding a glass of wine with a playful grin on his face. I can't help but start cracking up.

"What in the world are you doing?"

"Well, the wine is for you," he hands me the glass. "And the lack of clothing is me hoping it entices you to do the same. I think we should enforce a no clothing rule when you are in my apartment."

He starts laughing.

"How many drinks have you had?" I ask.

"I may have poured a third glass."

"You drunk fool. Come here," I wrap an arm around him and give him a kiss. When I pull away, I take a sip of wine. "I guess I need to catch up to you."

I sit down next to him and snuggle up under his arm as I take a sip of my wine.

"How does it feel to be an aunt?" he asks.

I smile at the thought of my niece Harper. It was so nice to be able to finally meet her and give her hugs and kisses. Becca had her wrapped up in a gorgeous floral blanket and she looked like sunshine swaddled up in flowers. Liam and Becca were the best team as they both listened to each other and helped one another. I just sat back and watched as they learned how to figure out their daughters needs for the first time.

"It's amazing! Harper is perfect," I tell him. "I can't wait to spoil her."

"I'm sure you're going to be her favorite. She's lucky to have an aunt like you."

I smile as I realize this man gets mushy when he is drunk.

"Thanks." I climb on top of him as I reach over to put my glass on the end table. "So, what had you so distracted at work that you had to come home early?"

He smiles up at me as I run my hands up and down his chest.

"I think it's this hot woman I have been sleeping with. I get all riled up just thinking about her at work that I can barely focus half the time."

He grabs my ass and starts to move me up and down over his body. I can feel him grow in his pants.

"How horrible for you. Maybe you need to get rid of her so you can focus."

He leans up until our lips are inches apart. "There's not a chance in hell of that happening."

Once our lips meet, we both sit up taller to bring our bodies together. His hands are in my hair as he increases the pressure of the kiss. After we break apart, he looks into my eyes. I can see his brain turning, like he cannot figure out what is happening between the two of us. He stands up from the couch and carries me through the hallway into his bedroom, where he lays me on the bed.

"You need to get these clothes off," he says as he starts undressing me until I'm down to just my underwear.

He begins trailing kisses down my body until he arrives between my legs. There has been some shift in the bedroom. The closer we get, the more intimate he seems to be during sex. I wonder if his dominant side was always a way to keep feelings out of the bedroom. Not that I mind that side of him, it's definitely a side that knows how to pull every ounce of pleasure from my body, but it's nice to see he can show a softer side as well.

He moves my panties to the side, looks up at me, and takes his first lick while holding his stare. He takes his time at first, making sure to slowly build up the pleasure. After he knows I'm squirming, he ditches the slow pace and devours me until I come in a frenzy on his mouth. Before I have a second to recover, he rolls on a condom, gets on his knees, places my feet on his shoulders and slams into me.

"Fuuuck, your pussy is so tight like this," he growls.

I want to respond but he is hitting parts of me I didn't know could be touched and all I can do is moan. When he picks up the pace, I begin panting and cursing over and over.

"Why can't I get enough of you?" he asks. "What is it about you?"

The questions seem to irritate him as he begins to get a bit rougher, grabbing my hips and slamming harder as my legs fall off of his shoulders and wrap around him. We are both moving our hips and meeting with each thrust, as sweat builds on our bodies. When he rubs his thumb over my clit, I go off like a rocket. He follows right behind me as he feels my walls squeeze him.

After he cleans himself up and we both dress, we lay back down in his bed. I'm enjoying the silence, when my phone, sitting on his nightstand, begins to ring.

"Uh, I'm way too relaxed to answer that," I mutter as I turn over and snuggle up to him. He wraps his arms around me.

"You've had a long day," he begins running soothing circles on my shoulder. These moments between us are becoming increasingly more frequent. The more times we are intimate, the longer we lay around together and hang out after. I wonder if he notices the change or if he would freak out if he realized the progression.

"Yeah, my mom had me running around with her all-around town. Now that we know it's a girl, she *needed* to go buy the baby girly clothes and blankets and you name it. I tried to convince her Becca and Liam have everything covered, but she wasn't having it." I laugh thinking of her so overjoyed, she couldn't sit down for a minute.

My phone rings again, which catches me off guard, but I assume it's just people calling to congratulate and ignore it again. When it rings a third time just a minute later, I begin to worry.

"I think you need to answer that," James says as he sits up. He reaches over his shoulder and retrieves my phone, handing it to me as he sits on the edge of the bed.

I look at it and see it is my mother. "Hello?"

I hear sniffling and my heart begins to beat faster. "Mom? What's going on? Are you okay?"

I look up at James, my eyes wide as I try to look at him for strength, not knowing what's coming. He reaches out and grabs my hand.

"Peyton," mom breaths out, barely audible. "It's Becca."

"What about Becca, Mom?"

Please, do not tell me something happened to Becca.

"She...," my mom struggles to speak through tears. "It's an amniotic fluid embolism. She's...gone Peyton. She's gone."

My body freezes. "What?" I choke out.

"She's gone. I just, I don't know what to do. We are at the hospital; Liam won't talk to anyone. How's he going to handle this?"

Tears build in my eyes and begin streaming down my cheeks. My body is responding to this news, but my brain can barely register anything besides the pain I feel in my heart. Becca... my friend, my sister. How could this have happened?

"Peyton, are you okay?" James pulls me out of my daze.

"Oh, mom," my cries take over. We both sit there on the phone, crying with each other.

After several minutes have passed, I try to collect myself.

"I'm coming to the hospital."

"No, dear. There's nothing you can do right now. We're here and Liam is in no shape to see anybody."

"I'll come for you," I argue.

"Honey, I have your father. Right now, I just need you to take care of yourself. Get some sleep and you can come over tomorrow. You're going to need your rest."

"Okay." I whisper.

"I'm going to go see if I can see the baby. Oh, they haven't even named her yet," she begins to cry.

"This isn't fair, Mom."

"No, it's not. Okay, I need to pull myself to together for Liam. Can you do me a favor and call your brothers to tell them? Please tell everyone not to come here tonight. Let your father and I be with Liam right now."

"Okay, Mom. I love you." The tears begin to fall again. "I'll see you tomorrow."

I hang up with my mom and my chest shakes as the pain takes over my body.

"Peyton, sweetheart." James wraps his arms around me.

I'm not sure how long I cry in his arms. He lets me lay on him until the tears will not come anymore.

"I'm sorry," I say as I sit up and try to compose myself.

"Why are you apologizing?" he asks. "Are you okay?"

"I don't know. It's...Becca, my sister-in-law. She had an embolism in the hospital, she didn't make it."

"Peyton, I'm so sorry." He takes me in his arms again. "What can I do?"

"Nothing. I'll go home; I know this is not part of our...arrangement. You don't need to see me like this."

"Hey, don't say that. We may have an odd... relationship," he seems to struggle to say the word. "But I care about you. And I want to help you, we *are* still friends."

Apparently, I didn't cry all my tears because a fresh new set begin to trickle down. I nod at his words because I'm afraid to speak and say something I shouldn't.

"Come on. Let's get you in the shower, you will feel much better."

I let him lead me to his bathroom where he turns on the shower and begins to undress me. I let him take each article of clothing off, thankful that my depleted body does not have to do the work. Next, he begins to remove his clothing until we are both naked. He takes my hand and leads me into the shower, both of us standing under the steady stream of hot water. The water burns my skin, making me feel human again, like I can feel something.

James grabs a bar of soap and starts to slowly wash my body as I stand there and let him take control. It feels so nice to let someone take care of me like this. For all the intimate things we have done together in bed, I feel the most exposed in this moment. Like he can see every part of me, the real me, and there is nothing I can do to hide.

When we finish, he hands me a towel and I manage to dry myself. Before I can get my clothes back on, he grabs me and softly gives me kisses.

"Stay with me tonight," he whispers. "I don't want you to be alone."

"James, you don't have to do this."

"I know I don't have to; I want to. I want to be there for you right now. Please, just don't argue with me."

"Okay," I say. "Thank you."

He gets boxers and a t-shirt for me to sleep in. Once we're both dressed, he turns the lights off and we slide under his covers. He wraps his arms around me and the feeling of security covers me. Deep down, I know this is dangerous for my heart, but I just don't have the energy to fight it. I quickly fall into a comfortable sleep.

Chapter Seventeen

James

When her breathing slows, I can tell she has drifted off to sleep. I can't explain what is making me take over like this, I just feel like she needs protecting, and I want to be the one to do it. I can't imagine what the family is going through right now, especially her brother Liam. To lose your wife before you even make it back home with your newborn baby. I know Peyton's family is close, this is going to be a huge loss for all of them.

I'm trying not to read into the driving force behind my desire to protect her. Right now, I'll just enjoy the fact that she is in my arms. I squeeze her a little tighter before I succumb to sleep.

I wake the following morning to Peyton slipping out of my arms. Her eyes are red and puffy, and she looks like she is on the verge of breaking down again.

"Good morning," she says while dressing.

"Morning," I get up and out of bed to stand in front of her.

"I'm sorry to wake you. I need to get to my parents' place. I'll call Lance and tell him I'm using vacation time."

I'm surprised she thinks I'm concerned about that at a time like this. "Hey, don't worry about that. How about we get some breakfast first?"

"I don't have time." I follow her out of my bedroom as she gathers her purse.

"Peyton, you need to take care of yourself first. Please, just let me get changed really fast and we can go grab something at the café on the first floor."

I see the internal debate she is having with herself right now. She is more worried about getting to her family, but I know her. Once she gets around them, she is going to forget about what she needs altogether. Before she has time to respond, I continue.

"You know what, I'm going to come with you. I'll change, we can grab food, and I will drive to your parents' house."

"What? James, no. You don't have to worry about me."

"I think I do. You're going to neglect yourself trying to take care of others, and I want to be there to take care of you. Besides, you're in no condition to drive right now. End of discussion, I'm coming with you. Just give me a minute."

I run into my bedroom to dress and freshen up as quickly as I can. Part of me is expecting her to have ditched me but she is standing there lost in her grief when I return. I hope that I'm doing the right thing by accompanying her.

"Okay, let's go." I grab my keys and we head out.

It only took us fifteen minutes to order breakfast and hop into my car. She gives me the address that I type into my GPS. It looks like her parents live about forty minutes away. That gave me time to call Lance and Angela to let them know we were not going to be in the office today and to slowly eat our breakfast in silence. I'm trying not to push her to talk right now. If she needs peace and quiet, that is what she will get.

When we pull into the driveway, I cut the engine. We sit there for a minute before I turn to her.

"You ready?" I ask.

She shakes her head back and forth. "When I walk through those doors, it becomes real. I'm not sure I'm ready for that."

I grab her hand. "I'm here for you. You are strong and brave; you can handle this."

I have absolutely no idea what I'm saying, I just hope it helps. This is entirely foreign territory for me.

I follow her lead and exit the car when she does. We continue up the front walkway, and it hits me. I'm about to meet the parents of the woman that I'm sleeping with. What in the world was I thinking? How are we going to explain our relationship? If she tells them I'm her boss, they are going to know something is going on. No one brings their boss to their house during a family tragedy.

Before I have time to ask her what we are going to say to her family, she opens the front door. We hear people rustling around and whispered voices as I follow her down a large hallway, filled with family pictures lining the walls. The photos are evidence of a lifetime of love that Peyton has been surrounded by. I'm willing to bet this is the first real tragedy this family has had to face.

We walk into the kitchen, and everyone stops talking as an older woman walks up to Peyton. She takes her into her arms, and they both cry. I stand there awkwardly, wondering what my role in this particular moment is, when a man approaches me, sticking out his hand for a shake.

"Hi, I'm Frank, Peyton's father." He takes my hand in a strong shake.

"James, Peyton's... friend," I say.

Friend seems like a good choice and it's the truth, we are friends. Peyton pulls out of her mother's arms and wipes the tears from her cheeks.

"I'm sorry. Mom, Dad, this is James."

I see a small smile form on her mother's lips, like perhaps she has heard about me.

"Hello, James. My name is Beverly."

"Nice to meet you," I shake her hand. "I'm so sorry about your loss."

Peyton takes my hand and leads me to the large kitchen island where there are three men looking at me skeptically, her brothers I assume.

"Guys this is James, a good friend of mine. He drove me here, so I wasn't distracted while driving," she turns to me. "James, these are my brothers Logan, Jackson, and Greyson."

"Nice to meet you, not under the circumstances. I'm truly sorry to hear about your loss."

"Nice to meet you. Thank you for driving Peyton," Greyson says.

"No problem at all. Whatever I can do to help."

"How do you know each other?" Jackson asks with a look of skepticism.

"We work together," Peyton interjects, clearly wanting to avoid that I am her boss.

Beverly ushers us all to sit down in the family room to talk about what the plan is.

"I'm going to do my best to get through this without crying," she says with a shaky voice. "We stayed with Liam for a while last night to figure out some details. Although it feels like time has stopped, life is still moving, and he still has a newborn baby to bring home today."

I hear Peyton sniffling next to me. When I look over at her, the pain etched on her face is so real that I feel a part of it in me.

"Liam needs to focus his time on getting to know his baby girl, so he agreed to let us work with Becca's parents to arrange the funeral. We will of course consult him whenever we feel necessary. Right now, he needs support from everyone. No matter how hard he tries, processing this loss will not happen for a while. He'll have too much to handle. I think your support will come in the form of helping with your niece. If he wants to talk about it, let him. However, let's follow his lead for now."

Everyone is nodding their head in agreement. I look over and see Frank running his hands through his hair, along his jaw, over his legs. I recognize those movements. He's trying to control his emotions right now.

"Harper will be released today around noon. I think we need to take shifts, so he's not alone in that house for a while. Peyton, I was thinking the womanly touch could be helpful for the first shift." Peyton nods her head. "If you could meet him at the hospital and drive home with him. You can stay with him until around eight. I would like to spend the first night with them to help him with the late-night feedings."

Everybody spends the next thirty minutes putting a schedule together for the next week while I watch on, stunned by the level of support they are willing to offer up to Liam. Even though he's going through his worst nightmare right now, he has a family that loves him and will give up everything to support him.

Moments later Peyton turns to me. "You can head home. I appreciate everything you have done, but it should just be Liam and me."

"Of course. How about I drop you off at the hospital and come pick you up at eight and drive you home?"

"That's too much."

I cut her off because I know where she is going. "It's not at all. You don't even have a car to get back home, and your family needs their rest."

She shakes her head. "Ok, thank you."

After I drop her off, I decide to head into the office to get some work done for a couple of hours.

Chapter Eighteen

Peyton

I am sitting on the couch holding my niece Harper. Harper was her mother's middle name. Liam thought of it yesterday at the hospital, I think it's perfect. Liam is holding up better than I thought he would be. Mom is right, he is focusing primarily on Harper right now. After we finished dinner, I told Liam to go upstairs to take a shower and relax for a little bit. Now that I'm alone, with Harper asleep in my arms, my mind keeps drifting to James. The way he held me last night, insisted on me sleeping over, and taking me home this morning. It's a big shift in our relationship, or whatever it's we have together. I feel like I need to have a talk with him about what we're doing. I'm beginning to feel things for him, things that will lead to a broken heart if I'm not careful.

I look down at my phone when it vibrates to see a text from James.

James: On my way, be there in thirty.

Liam comes down a couple minutes later looking a bit more refreshed.

"Hey, you look good."

"I feel a bit better. How's she doing?" he asks as he takes a seat next to me. We both look down at her innocent face as she sleeps.

"Perfect. She's absolutely perfect."

"Just like her mom," Liam whispers before he looks up at me. "How am I going to do this, Peyton?"

"You're going to be a great father. It will take some time to get the hang of it, but you're not alone. We're all here for you. This doesn't all fall on you. We're a family, and we help each other out."

"Why did it have to be her?" he says as his eyes begin to glisten. I hate to see him like this. I can't help the tears that fall from my face. I know I'm supposed to be strong for him and let him cry to me, but the pain is real for me as well.

"I don't know. Do we ever know why things happen? The most we can do is be thankful for the times we had with someone and live our lives in a way that they would be proud of."

"That's what I will do. I will be the father that Becca would be proud of."

I grab his hand and he gives it a squeeze, telling me he has got this. I know Liam, this will not break him. The sound of the front door opening breaks the moment.

"Hello?" my mother calls from the foyer.

"In the family room," Liam shouts, startling Harper. She scrunches up her face and begins to cry just as my mom is walking in. Liam goes to grab her but my mother all but lunges for Harper.

"No,no,no. You sit right back down. I'll take her, it's my fault she is crying."

After I pass her off to mom, I look down at my phone and see that James will be here any minute. I begin to gather my things and start to say my goodbyes to Liam and Mom, telling them that I will see them soon. Just as I am putting my shoes on, I see the headlights turn into the driveway. I walk outside and let myself into the passenger's seat. He puts the car and reverse and begins backing out of the driveway.

"How did it go?" he asks.

"It was really good. I'm happy I got that time alone with Liam. It helped me see that he is strong enough to handle this. He has a good head on his shoulders. He will need our help, but he can do it."

James reaches over and squeezes my thigh. "I'm glad you got to see that for yourself. It'll make it easier for you to leave him, knowing that you have faith in him."

When I lean my head back against his leather seat, I let out a sigh. "I agree," I look over at him. "Thank you for...everything you've done. It's been really nice having someone to talk to about this."

"I'm happy to help, Peyton."

James pulls up to a parking spot outside of my apartment and puts the car in park.

"Come here," he whispers as he leans over. He grabs my face and kisses me long and slow. Every thought escapes me as I melt into the tenderness of this kiss, to the feel of his soft lips slightly increasing their pressure over mine. When he stops and pulls away, it takes me a second to recover. "Tell me what you want me to do. If you're tired and need some alone time, I'm okay with that. If you want some company, I would be happy to come up."

I should tell him I need to be alone. Spending this much time together is messing with me, but I am too greedy and want to spend time with him.

"Come up. I would love the company."

The smile that spread across his face makes me ache. Is he feeling this too?

"Well, let's get going," he turns off his car.

Once we are in my apartment, I tell him to make himself comfortable while I go take a shower. Once I'm done, I join him on the couch while I brush my hair.

"ESPN? Do you ever watch anything else?"

"I honestly don't watch much television. I guess not until the last couple of months." He eyes me suggestively.

"Are you trying to say that I'm the reason you are watching more television?"

He shrugs his shoulders. "You're the only explanation I can make of it. I guess since you have come around, I have possibly learned to chill out a bit and not work myself to the bone."

"I'm not sure I'm the best example if you are trying to learn how to work less."

"Maybe not, but you're still better at it than I am."

I put my brush down on the end table and snuggle into his side. "Can I convince you to try out a show with me?"

"Did you have a specific show in mind?"

He adjusts his arm and wraps it around my shoulders, bringing me closer.

"I wanted to watch this show called Manifest. It might actually take my mind off of everything right now."

"Go for it," he tells me.

We settle into the first episode, and I get sucked into the storyline. I'm surprised that I feel a bit better when the show ends. Before we get sucked into another episode, I turn off the tv and stand up.

"You ready for bed?" I hold out my hand for him. He takes it as I lead him to my bedroom. When we reach my bed, I turn around and look up into his eyes. Standing up on my tippy toes, I kiss his soft lips with more emotion behind it than I ever have put into it. He responds back with a soft, slow kiss that sends shivers throughout my body.

"Thank you, James," I whisper in between kisses. He slowly strips my clothes off before he reaches behind his back to lift off his shirt. Will I ever tire of seeing his body on display? I can't help but reach out and slowly move my hands up and down his chest and abs. I step closer to place my lips on his chest as I slowly kiss down his body. Licking between all the crevices on his stomach. I hear him pull in a sharp breath as my tongue continues to glide further down. When I get to my knees and look up at him, his eyes are hooded from his desire.

He only lets me taste him for a second before he pushes me onto the bed and kisses me again with the same passion and emotion as before. There's something different between us right now. He's going slow; I feel him telling me something in his every move. Telling me he is feeling more for me. When he puts on the condom and pushes inside me, his eyes never part from mine as he pulls out slowly and gives a little push back in. He keeps a steady rhythm but is not in a hurry. The eye contact is what eventually does me in and has me falling apart as he follows me seconds later.

We lay there in each other's arms for a while before he finally speaks.

"It's late and we have to be up early tomorrow. I don't have any clothes for work tomorrow, I should probably head home." He gets up and puts his clothes on as he comes over to my side of the bed, pulling the covers up over my shoulders. He leans in to give me a kiss but stops short.

"Shoot, I was going to tuck you in, but I just realized you need to lock the door before I leave."

The thought of getting out of bed sounds like too much work, my body is begging me to let it rest. Maybe it's the desire to stay put that leads me to say what I tell James next.

"Mmm, I don't want to get up. You can just take the spare key and lock up. It's hanging on the key rack by the door on a Chicago keychain."

He goes stiff for a second, likely surprised by my suggestion, but recovers quickly. He leans in gives me a quick kiss on the lips.

"No problem. You just stay put and get some rest; I'll see you in the office tomorrow."

Once I hear the door shut, sleep takes over. I'm thankful for this because I do not want to lay here and analyze why I just gave James a key to my apartment.

Chapter Nineteen

James

It's Saturday afternoon, and I've just been convinced to meet all of Peyton's family at her parents' house. I went to the funeral service this morning thinking I would give my condolences and leave. Her mother got to me before I could leave and told me it would mean a lot to Peyton if I went to the burial. I had no idea if that were true, nor how to say no to the lady, so I agreed. After the burial, as soon as I reached my car, Beverly stopped me again.

"Thank you for supporting Peyton through this difficult time," she adds as we watch Peyton hold her niece while talking to her brothers.

"It's no problem at all. She's a good friend."

"Is that all that you two are, friends?" Her eyebrows peak up over her sunglasses.

I'm not sure how to respond. Of course, we are more than friends. However, friends who are just having sex does not sound like the right thing to say to her mother, so I am forced to settle with just friends.

"Yes, we're just friends. She is a great employee. I'm happy to help her in any way that I can."

"I see," she says the doubt evident in her tone. "Well, friends it is. She will be happy to have her *friend* there to support her. We will see you back at the house."

Did she just call my bullshit? The way she said *friend* suggested I'm full of crap. I just didn't expect her to all but call me on it.

Beverly walks over to Peyton and whispers in her ear making Peyton quickly look my way. She shakes her head and gives the baby over to her mother than heads my way. When she reaches me to huffs out a breath of frustration.

"I'm sorry if my mother just guilted you into coming over. You don't have to come if you don't want to."

"She didn't guilt me at all. I would be happy to come and spend time with you. Besides, I already told her I would come, I can't back out now. That would put me on her bad side. We don't want that."

"I suppose so," she says as she looks down at the ground.

"Come on, ride with me. Keep me company."

"Okay." She follows me to the passenger side and takes a seat after I open the door for her.

We're driving in silence when I hear her sniffling next to me. I reach over for her hand, she squeezes tightly.

"It's going to get easier," I say in an effort to soothe her.

"I know," she whispers. "Whether it gets easier or not, doesn't make it fair."

"It certainly doesn't. She will always grow up with a missing piece to her soul. I know from experience."

She looks over at me and I feel like she can see through all of my layers. All the walls that I put up to protect myself. We finish the ride in silence as I try to control these feelings that seem to consume me. I feel like I'm losing control of our relationship and don't know what to do.

When we walk into her parent's house, we hear chattering coming from the kitchen. Everyone is standing around the island pouring drinks and talking. We're offered a beer and glass of a wine, as I pull out a seat for Peyton to take at the island. I settle in standing next to her. Everyone has begun reminiscing about their favorite Becca memories. Jackson is telling an animated story about the first time he met her, he didn't know she was Liam's girlfriend, and he hit on her.

"Why does that not surprise me?" Beverly says as everyone laughs.

After an hour of stories, people begin to get into their own conversations. I'm currently talking to Frank about the business and how I got into it. He is a businessman himself and turns out to be a decent person to run ideas by. He's been through countless mergers and software changes himself, understanding the stress they can put on leadership. I end up having a good time with her family, suddenly a bit jealous that I never had this kind of support in my life. I'm usually not close enough to anyone to meet their families, so I don't have to witness what I lost.

"Janice's son Max is single now, you two should go out," I overhear Beverly say tell Peyton.

My first reaction is to tense up as I wait for Peyton's answer. My hand is clutching my beer bottle so hard, I fear it may shatter. It's not like I can interject and turn down the idea. I just told her hours ago that Peyton and I are just friends. Everything in me wants to take it all back and claim her as mine. It certainly feels like she is mine. The thought of anyone else having her makes me want to punch someone.

"Mom," Peyton looks at me shocked, before she turns back to her mother. "I don't think that's an appropriate thing to ask me."

"Why not dear? You *are* single, I don't see the harm." She has a knowing smile on her face. What if Peyton agrees to it? Will that be the end of us? I feel myself begin to sweat at the idea.

"Mom let's discuss this another time," Peyton narrows her eyes.

"Why don't we all head outside to the patio," Frank suggests as he smirks at me.

Just as everyone is refilling their drinks and heading outside, I look over at Liam as he comes downstairs with Harper, now changed out of her dress into comfy looking clothes. He looks rough, I can only imagine what he is going through. I don't know much about babies, but I know enough that doing it on your own when just losing your wife is a personal hell for anyone.

Beverly comes back in and grabs Harper from Liam.

"Hi, my sweet girl," she kisses her cheek. "Come with Grand-ma, let's give your daddy a break." She looks at Liam. "You go rest, I will watch her for a while."

"I think I'll go outside with every." Beverly looks surprised at his response.

"It's okay if you don't want to...," Liam cuts her off.

"Mom, I just can't be alone with my thoughts right now." She nods her head before she walks off with Harper.

Later in the evening, Peyton and I are driving back to her place when she brings up her mother's question.

"I'm sorry about what my mother said. She was just trying to be sneaky and get us to admit something is going on between us. Well, she knows something is going on, but she doesn't understand why it's a secret."

"What do you mean, she knows?"

"Well, Becca sort of got it out of me while mom was right there. And she kind of guessed as well."

I nod my head at I drive, reluctant to continue with this conversation.

"Yeah." Peyton gets quiet for a second as she looks out the window. "Maybe we should talk about us though. What are we doing here, James? We're more than just friends, but what exactly are we?"

I was not ready for this question. It catches me off guard. Why is she bringing this up? I thought we were enjoying what was happening between us.

"I don't know, Peyton!" I raise my voice with annoyance.

"It's a valid question, James!" she shouts back.

"I just, ugh...," I punch the steering wheel in frustration. "I told you from the beginning what this could be. None of that has changed."

"Excuse me? Did you say nothing has changed? We spend all of our time together; we even sleep at each other's place now. You came to my sister in law's funeral. You even came back to my parent's house, and don't you DARE blame that on my mother. You could have *easily* declined her offer."

"I was trying to be respectful; she just lost her daughter-in-law."

"You're going to tell me your feelings for me have not grown at all? That what we have been doing together is exactly what you intended from the beginning?" I can feel her anger emanating through the car.

"Of course, I care about you, we're friends." She laughs at that statement, but I continue. "We're spending more time together than I had originally foreseen, but I told you from the beginning we could never be more. I'm not capable of more. I can't give you everything that you need."

I pull up to the curb outside of her apartment and put the car in park. We sit there in silence, neither of us knowing what to say to each other.

"I feel more for you. I'm...falling for you," she whispers. I look over at her and see a tear fall down her cheek and can barely swallow past the lump forming in my throat. She looks so beautiful right now. All I want to do is reach out and grab her hand, but I stop myself. I can't let myself get her hopes up, or mine. I will only end up disappointing her in the end.

"I'm so fucking sorry, Peyton. I didn't mean for it to get to this point. I... got carried away."

She laughs at my words as tears continue to roll down her cheeks. "So, I'm the only one feeling this."

I'm feeling it too. Shit, of course I am. I have not allowed myself to admit it or let myself take the time to see it, but how could I not be feeling that way towards her? She's fucking perfect, everything I would want in a woman. She takes my silence as an admission that she is correct, that I don't feel the same way she does. She opens her door to get out of the car. I want to stop her, to beg her to tell me that I am enough to make her happy, but that would take admitting my greatest fault. I just can't bear to see the disappointment in her eyes if I tell her, so I let her go.

Chapter Twenty

Peyton

He didn't deny it. When I said that I was the only one falling in love, he didn't tell me that I was wrong. He just sat there in silence, probably too afraid to hurt my feelings. To tell me to my face that he didn't love me. I just made it back to into my apartment ten minutes ago and have been crying on my couch. I didn't know who to call for the first five minutes. Eventually, I grabbed my phone to call Becca and when my brain caught up, it hit me even harder. She's no longer there to listen to or get advice from.

After about an hour, I picked myself up off the floor and got in the shower. Just when I was getting into bed, ready to sleep the rest of the evening away, I get a message from Blake.

Blake: Hey girl. Sorry, I had to run out after the funeral, I wasn't feeling well.

She has recently been tied up in a weird relationship with her neighbor, Sam. Right now, they are on the rocks. I don't want to unload my drama on her, but I need someone to talk to. We have kept in touch throughout my time with James. She met him again at the funeral and I can tell she was excited that he came. She kept on looking at us while smiling. I pick up the phone and give her a call.

"Hey. How are you doing?" she answers.

Before I have time to answer, the tears begin again.

"Peyton, are you crying?" I sniff at the question. "Oh, honey. I know, I'm so sorry. I know how close Becca and you were."

"It's not...just... that," I say between sobs.

"What is it?" she asks with concern.

"It's James. He...we...ended things. I told him I was falling for him, and he got mad. He said he laid out what this was from the start."

"Peyton, I'm so sorry! I figured when he was so involved this past week, that things were taking a turn and getting serious."

"I don't know what happened. I guess I got confused when we started spending so much time together and he came to my parent's house. I let myself believe he was feeling the same. It's my fault, he did tell me what we were from the beginning."

"Absolutely not!" she fires back. "You don't do the things he did for you if you are just screwing around in the sheets. He clearly has feelings for you."

"Even if that were true, I don't see him admitting to it."

"That's his loss. You know that, right?"

"I guess. I just wish it were different."

"You know what? I bet he comes around. You probably just caught him off guard. Give him a chance to think it over."

I doubt that will happen, but I agree with her to appease her. Once we say our goodbyes, I turn off my light.

I've known for a while that I was developing real feeling for James. I guess a part of me thought he was feeling the same things too. Why would he have done half the things he did if he wasn't? Was it pity? And why does he keep telling me he would let me down, that he wasn't enough for me? Eventually, I fall asleep without any answer to these questions.

Monday morning, after no word from James the rest of the weekend, I go into work with my head held high. I will not let him treat me this way, making me feel unloved or underappreciated. I wear my sexiest red work dress, style my hair with just the right amount of wave, and add tall, cream heals in the mix. We have a meeting around ten with the developers and consultants to go over the final details of the first roll out.

I'm the first one to the meeting to lay out all the folders and put out the water. Just as I'm taking a seat, James walks in, looking tired and worn out, like he hasn't slept much. I almost feel bad until I get an image of him drinking and spending his evenings with one of the whores at the club, then I get *pissed*.

"Peyton," he says quietly. "I've been wanting to call you all weekend, I just didn't know what to say."

He takes a seat and runs both hands over his face. Before he continues, I cut him off.

"Don't bother. Let's just keep this professional and leave our past relationship out of it." I find a seat at the opposite end of the table from him.

"Did you say *past* relationship? What the hell does that mean?"

"Oh, please. I have more pride than to stay involved with you. You don't expect me to keep sleeping with you after pouring my heart out and getting nothing in return?" I try not to shout but I know my voice is getting too loud.

"I... guess I thought we would talk about it and... shit. I don't know." He runs a frustrated hand through his hair. Thankfully, I'm saved from this conversation as the consultants begin to file into the meeting room.

We spend the next two hours going over the details. James is moody and snapping at everyone the entire meeting. I try to ignore anytime he speaks, but he keeps trying to address me directly and it is getting on my last nerve. Once the meeting is over, we begin filing out and I almost run to the elevators to escape James. Luckily, he does not follow me to my office, but I do receive a text message about an hour later.

James: I'm sorry. Can we please talk later?

What the hell am I supposed to do with that? I focus on getting some of my work done for a while before I give in and answer him.

Me: Fine.

I may as well give him the time to say what he needs to say so he will leave me alone. He answers back almost immediately.

James: Can you come up to my office in thirty minutes?

I thought he meant after work. On second thought, maybe it's best if we have this conversation at work. If we're going to be strictly professional from here on out, I'll have to get used to that.

Me: I'll be there.

I stand outside his office door, taking in a deep breath before I knock. Once I finally gain the courage, which is more to do with not wanting Angela to see me standing outside his door like a fool, I lift my hand to the door and knock.

"Come in," he shouts.

I open the door as he stands from his chair in his dark blue suit. He meets me at the other side of his desk. We both stand there looking at each other and I can feel it, I can the pull between us. He leans down and offers a quick kiss to my cheek. I almost cry right there, feeling the awkwardness that's already there.

"Thanks for coming," he says. "Let's go sit on the sofa."

We walk over to his brown leather sofa, which I realize we have never used before. He waits for me to take a seat then sits next to me, leaning his elbows on his knees.

"It's no problem. I suppose we need to hash this out."

"I just wanted to apologize for how I acted last night. I was caught off guard and did not react well."

"That's fair." He was caught off guard, but that does not change how he feels.

"I have a history, a dark one. It's not one that I'm proud of, but I just wanted you to know that none of this has anything to do with you. I think you're amazing! I do care for you, but I still can't give you what you need."

I hate hearing the same excuse a thousand different ways. It still sounds to me like he is running from something.

"Why do you keep saying that? What is it that you can't give me?"

"It doesn't matter. You just need to trust me."

"What the hell kind of explanation is that? Don't you think I deserve the truth?"

"Peyton, I'm giving you the best I can here. Please, try to understand."

His head hangs between his shoulders as he massages the back of his neck. I would feel bad if he weren't breaking my heart in the vaguest way imaginable.

"I don't understand. I don't know how we can share the hard-est week of my life together. You support me like no one else ever has before, and yet you can't open up to me enough to tell me what it is that's keeping us apart."

My emotions are bubbling to the surface, and I can't fight the tears that come. I have cried more in this past week than I have in my life.

"I don't talk about this with anyone, it's not just you," he says, like that is supposed to make me feel better.

"Well, that might be part of your problem," I reply.

He nods his head in agreement but does not offer any response.

I eventually continue, realizing he has nothing else to say. "If you ever feel like talking about it, I'll be around. Until then, let's keep our interactions to strictly professional."

Chapter Twenty-One

James

"Dude, you look like shit," Greg says across from me at the bar. I take a big swig from my draft beer to try to take the edge off. "Thanks, man."

"What's going on? Is work getting crazy?"

"Nah, work is fine." Work has been the only thing lately that has been keeping me from completely losing my mind.

"Well, then what gives? You seem depressed."

"It's nothing that I want to get into right now."

"Fair enough. Well, I'm glad you called, it's been too long."

This past week without Peyton has been miserable. It's never been this hard to stay away from a woman before. For the first time in a long time, I was enjoying life. I wasn't going through the motions. When I lay down in bed and close my eyes, I see her smiling face and can hear her laugh, and my chest aches.

"Yeah, sorry about that."

"No worries. Tell me, how's your girl?"

My face must give me away because his expression changes to a knowing, sympathetic smile.

"Ahhh, now I see the reason for the mood," he says before taking a sip of his beer. "What happened?"

I give him a brief description of what has played out in the last couple weeks. I never have been one to talk about myself. Giving him the details feels foreign to me, but he sits there in interest as he nods along listening to my miserable life.

"It's my fault. There's a reason I go to the club. Shit always gets too real and feelings get hurt."

"Ha! You think that's why you go to the club?" He shakes his head at me like I just told a hilarious joke, not like I just bared my pain to him.

"What the fuck does that mean?"

"It means, you are in denial man. You go to the club because you are too afraid to open yourself up to getting hurt again. You play it off that you don't want to hurt these women, but it's *you* who doesn't want to get hurt."

My first reaction to his words is to get pissed. How dare he pretend to know the reasons behind my decisions.

"Really? You're going to fucking pretend like you know me that well. No one knows all my reasons for my decisions."

"Yeah, because you keep everyone out. Maybe if you opened up to me, I could help you. Peyton was a catch, and I can tell you were crazy about her. Don't let her get away because you are afraid."

"I've had enough of this conversation."

He seems to pick up on how close I am to snapping and agrees to let it go the rest of the evening. When I get back home that night, his words are on replay in my head as I lay in bed. Am I in denial about the real reasons I have stayed away from any real relationship? Did Margaret offer the final blow that closed me off to women for good?

Sitting in this conference room is the biggest form of torture. Watching Peyton talk to the consultants and work her magic, knowing I can never have her again. I've spent this entire meeting lost in the soothing rhythm of her voice, wishing I could grab her and bring her to my office to get another taste of those luscious lips. Her high ponytail is just begging for me to grab it. It's like she knows where my weaknesses are and tries to use them against me.

After what feels like the longest meeting of my life, everyone begins to file out. I stay put in my seat as Peyton begins to clean up and close down her computer.

"You were quiet today," she says as she stands up and places everything in her bag. She is acting like nothing has happened between us and it's pissing me off. I stand from my chair and make large strides until I am inches from her. Towering over her, I look at this beauty who has me all mixed up.

"I'm trying my hardest not to want you, but it's not working. You were all I could think about during that meeting." I grab her ponytail and yank her head, so she is looking up at me. "You and this damn ponytail are making me want to do things to you that I'm not allowed to do anymore."

She makes an audible gulp as her gaze turns dark. I know this is wrong, yet I can't help myself from leaning in. The taste of her lips is the only thing that can soothe this ache. When I'm centimeters away, she glances at the floor while shaking her head.

"James, please stop." She begins to back up, putting enough distance between us so that I can no longer touch her. "This isn't going to make anything easier for us. Nothing has changed."

With that, she grabs her bag and walks out of the room, leaving me alone. Memories from my past keep flooding in as I fall to the chair next to me. I see myself alone in foster homes with no one to love me, alone at my parent's funeral with no one to take me home, and alone at the doctor's office. The doctor's office, where I found out that the abuse that I suffered in foster care had led to damage that will prevent me from ever becoming a father, the real reason Margaret left me. I can hear her yelling at me while she packed her bags. Telling me she *didn't sign up for this kind of life*. One where she could not be a mother. She was angry at me, stating that I ruined our life together and I will never be enough for anyone. I need these memories to go away.

It's only three o'clock, but I can't stay in the office for another minute longer. I rush to my office to close everything down and tell Angela that I'm done for the day. As soon as I make it to the streets, I lean my hands against my knees, trying to contain the storm building inside of me. I need a drink; I need many drinks. Whatever will keep these feelings from taking over.

I don't know how long I have been sitting at this bar drinking. When I look outside, I see the sun going down. The threat of the nighttime approaching and the loneliness grabbing a hold of me is too much. I pay my tab and am approaching Peyton's apartment before I can convince myself how stupid of an idea this is. I am sick and tired of feeling like I am in this fight alone. For once, I want someone to know why I'm the way that I am. I want to be able to give Peyton the truth.

When I get to her place, I look down and see it is eight. I must have been at the bar for almost five hours, and I feel it. It takes me a minute to find Peyton's name on the intercom since everything is a bit blurry. I hit the button and wait a minute, hoping she is home. I almost give up and go home but as I turn around to leave, I hear the buzzer as the door unlocks.

Chapter Twenty-Two

Peyton

"How's he doing?" I ask my mom as I sit on my couch, dressed in my cozy pajamas.

"Now that he is settled with Harper, I think the loss of Becca is starting to really hit him. Sometimes I see him looking right through Harper, like his mind is somewhere else."

"I hate this, Mom. Why did it have to happen? I miss her so much." I try to blink away the tears, managing somewhat successfully to keep my composure.

"I've learned a long time ago that we are not meant to understand why. The only thing we can do is trust that God had a plan, and everything is working out how it should."

That is a bitter pill to swallow. I don't know how Liam and Harper going through life without Becca is part of a bigger plan because to me, it feels wrong.

"I'm so glad you have James through all of this," Mom says.

I've tried to avoid this discussion with my family. They have enough on their plate without adding my silly little broken heart. But sitting here by myself, when I would normally be in his arms, is too much to bear alone.

"Mom, James and I...we are not together anymore."

"What?" she almost shouts. "How could that be? I know what I saw between you two. Not that I have any idea why either of you wouldn't just admit it."

"Because we were never anything more than friends having fun together, at least to him. He warned me from the beginning, he does not do relationships. And I stupidly went and fell in love with him. Once I told him, he freaked out."

"Oh, that silly man. Of course, he's in love with you too. Trust me, a mother knows these things."

"Well, if he were, I think we'd be together right now."

"Give it time, sweetheart."

Suddenly, my intercom buzzes. When I get up to see who is there, I see James and my heart immediately leaps in his chest. What is he doing here? I'm equal parts excited and terrified.

"Mom, I gotta go. Someone just rang my buzzer."

By the time I disconnect with my mom, he is knocking on my door. I try to take deep breathes to calm my nerves before I open the door. He's standing there, still in his suit from work, looking every bit as sexy as he always does. Yet there is a sadness to him, one that was not always there.

"Hi," is all I can up with right now.

"Can I come in?" he barely meets my eyes with the question.

"Sure," I hold the door open. He stumbles a bit as he crosses the room, I think he may be drunk.

When I join him on the couch, I smell the alcohol on him. His eyes are glassy, and he looks tired. Why is he doing this to himself, to us, if it is so hard for him? We continue to sit there for a couple minutes before he begins to fidget in his seat. I can tell he is nervous, but I'm not going to be the one to force anything out of him. If he came here to tell me something, he can say it when he is ready.

"Peyton, I...I don't know why I came here. I just had to see you."

Anger radiates throughout my body at his admission. I'm not going to be pushed around like this. It's not fair to me for him to keep pushing these boundaries every time he misses me. How does he not realize how much he is breaking my heart?

"No!" I leap off the couch, not able to sit down with this much adrenaline coursing through me. "You do *not* get to come here and tell me you miss me. My heart isn't a toy, and this is not a game."

"I'm sorry!" he stands. "I don't want to do this to you, but I can't stay away. I need you... I...I *love* you!"

"You what? You love me? How dare you say that! Why are you doing this to me? If you love me, why can't we be together?"

"I'm no good for you!" he falls back down to the couch. "I can't give you what you need."

"What the hell does that even mean? I'm so sick of hearing that damn excuse! Because that's all it is, an excuse!"

"No, it's not!" he screams. "I'll never be able to give any woman what they deserve! I can't have children, okay? My foster parent beat the shit out of me one night and one swift kick to the groin took away any chance of me becoming a father."

All that anger and rage that I was feeling is gone in an instant, replaced with sadness. Sadness for this man, crumbling in front of me as he comes to terms with his past. A past that no one should ever have had to endure. I join him on the couch and reach out to place my hand on his knee.

"James, I... I'm so sorry."

He keeps his head down, like looking at me is too much for him right now. "I didn't even know for most of my life. They put it in my chart at the hospital the night it happened; I was ten. But I guess no one thought a ten-year-old needed to hear that news on top of everything else. And it's not like I had parents to remember to break the news to me one day. So, I lived my life. Was finally placed in a great foster home, made it to college, and met someone. We fell in love and got engaged. It wasn't until one day when I got in an accident and landed in the hospital that things changed. The doctor was looking through my charts and happened to bring up that little detail. I could tell right there that Margaret was shocked, but I thought we would get home and talk about our options. She knew right away she couldn't marry me, told me that I was never going to be able to offer her what she deserved, what any woman deserved. She packed her things that night, gave me the ring, and moved out."

Fury, absolute fury is what I feel towards his ex-fiancé. How could she not even give it time to sit down and talk through their options? That doesn't sound like love to me. She sounds like a selfish bitch, only looking out for herself. James dodged a bullet with that one. No marriage can be successful if one person is only looking out for themselves. Right now, James needs my compassion though. Not for me to bad talk his ex.

"James, that is awful. I'm so sorry you had to go through that. I'm sorry that evil man took something so precious away from you."

He shrugs his shoulders, like it's no big deal. "What can I do? It happened, and it's part of who I am."

"I know that, I know you can't change the past. But you're aloud to feel angry for what you have been through. You can feel angry at what that man did to you."

"What's the point?"

"To work through it. So, you can get to a point where you are okay with your past and who you are today. Keeping this inside and not telling anyone is not healthy."

"Oh, yeah, work through it? Tell me, do you want to stay with me now? Knowing we could never have a child of our own together?"

I'm stunned by his question, but the answer won't come. I know I should tell him nothing could stop me from wanting to be with him. I should tell him that this doesn't define who he is and whether he is worthy of love. I should say a lot of this and more, but I say nothing.

He chuckles at my silence. "That's what I thought. You don't want to hurt me, you want me to be happy and proud of who I am, but you can't tell me that this doesn't change things for you."

"That's not fair, you just came in here and told me this minutes ago. I need time to process it. Up until you showed up, you led me to believe that we were over. That you were not in love with me. Now, you come here and say you love me. It's a lot to process."

He stands up and begins to rush towards my front door. "This was a bad idea."

"James don't leave!" I say as I follow him.

"Well, now you know my secret. Now you know my flaws. Hope this makes it easier for you to move on." I see the tears forming in his eyes and my heart is breaking.

"Please," I whisper. "Let's just talk about this."

The door slams in my face and I fall to the floor in tears. I hate myself for not being able to say those words to him, to tell him that it doesn't change anything for me. I wasn't expecting to have to decide my entire future in the blink of an eye to a man that was telling me he loved me for the first time while drunk. Nothing seems fair in this moment.

Chapter Twenty-Three

Peyton

Today is Blake's fourth of July party that she is throwing at her new house. Everything in me wants to cancel and stay home to drink and eat my sorrows away but Blake has been going through her own struggles. I need to be there for her as her friend. I throw on a pair of cut off shorts and a red tank top and drive out to her house. When I get there, I go into full on helper mode as I try to assist in getting trays of food ready. This helps me keep my mind off of James, so I try to stay in the kitchen most of the afternoon.

I've just brought out yet another tray of appetizers when I hear an ambulance outside. I figure it must be the neighbors until I walk back into the kitchen and see the lights are just outside of Blake's house. I run outside and see Blake on a stretcher heading towards the ambulance with her sort of boyfriend Sam by her side.

"Blake!" I yell as I run towards her. When I reach the back of the ambulance, I see her laying there unconscious and my heart about stops beating. "Oh my gosh! What happened?"

"I don't know! I followed her upstairs and when I found her in the bathroom, she was passed out on the floor. I couldn't wake her up," Sam responds.

"Oh my gosh!" I begin pacing back and forth. I don't think I can take losing anyone else in my life right now.

"Look, I'm going to ride with her. Why don't you meet us at the hospital?" Sam says as he hops into the back of the ambulance.

I nod my head in agreement since words are lost on me.

Half an hour later, Sam and I are sitting in the waiting room when the doctor comes out. We spring from our seats as he makes his way in our direction.

"Are you here for Blake Morgan?" he asks.

"Yes," we say in unison.

"Blake is doing just fine. She is awake and stable."

The breath that I had been holding can finally be released as relief floods my body.

"Fainting is a common side effect in the first trimester," the doctor says, and I lose track of what he is saying. Blake is pregnant? How could I not know this? Based on the stunned look on Sam's face, I am guessing he had no idea he was going to be a father. I tell Sam to go see her first while I go make a phone call to her mother.

The next few hours pass by in a blur as we meet with her and make sure she is okay. Sure enough, she knew she was pregnant but had not told anybody yet. I can't believe this is happening, a baby. As I'm driving back home, my mind drifts to James. If we were together, I would never know the joys of finding out that we created a baby together. Can I give that up to be with him? I know that if I decide to try to be with him, to fight him in his stubbornness to stay away, I need to be one hundred percent sure that I am willing to give that dream up. He deserves that after everything life has thrown at him.

When I get home that night, I begin to look into options for a couple when the male is sterile. I happen upon stories from husbands and wives telling their heartbreaking stories about their failed attempts to get pregnant. An hour later, I'm sitting behind my laptop with tears running down my face as I read in depth stories about the pain and suffering the males can face when they are the ones who cannot contribute to making a baby. They feel like less of a man, like something is wrong with them, like they did something wrong in life to deserve this. It breaks my heart thinking of James sitting there with these kinds of feelings.

As I continue to scroll through, I find a particular story about a couple who took their situation and adopted. They gave these young lives a second chance at a happy family. There are pictures of the family at important events throughout the kids' lives and you can see the joy in everyone's face. They were a family, they had each other, and they were not lacking in love or happiness.

The next is a story about a couple who chose the route of a sperm donor. The father wrote about how he felt at first, like he wasn't a valuable part of the process with their first child. But after he held the baby for the first time, he knew that he would love the child exactly like he would if he were the biological father.

I close my eyes and picture what it would be like to have James holding our baby for the first time in the hospital and everything in me knew that it just felt *right*. I know it all sounds so crazy! We hadn't even been a real couple, and I'm already considering having a family with him. I know what it would look like from the outside, but I don't care! I want to be with him, to be the one to show him how much he can give and how happy he could make me. Before I can talk myself out of it, I'm changing my clothes and dashing out the door towards his apartment.

On my way, I realize it's the holiday weekend and the chances of him being home are slim to none. I reach into my bag and take out my phone to text him.

Me: Are you home right now?

I don't expect him to answer which is why I'm surprised when I hear the buzz of my phone only minutes later.

James: I am.

I can't help but smile at his blunt and no-frills answer.

Me: I am on my way. Be there in five.

After the longest five minutes of my life, I hop out of the cab and rush towards the elevator. The ride up to the top floor is enough time for me to realize how *insane* I am right now. It's too late to turn back now, so when the doors open, I step out and knock on his door.

Chapter Twenty-Four

James

I open the door and see Peyton standing there in jean shorts and a tank top. Her smile lights up while I stand there in confusion, wondering why she's so happy to see me. I should be the last person to put such a look on her face. After a minute of us just standing there, she raises her eyebrows at me.

"Oh, uh sorry. Please come on in," I stutter out like a fool as I open the door for her to walk through. "Would you, uh, like something to drink?"

How can my heart hurt so much just by being near her? I feel like I'm going against every cell in my body by not taking her in my arms. I have to actively remind myself that she's no longer mine to touch, to love. Because I know now without a doubt, that I love her. I have been so miserable without her these last couple weeks. Everything seems dull and gray without her in my life. Not that it was all sunshine and roses before she entered.

"I'm sorry," she blurts out.

"What?" I ask in confusion. What could she possibly have to be sorry about?

"I'm so sorry for taking so long to come to you. I was scared and confused. It's all a lot to take in, but I know what I want now. I don't care if you can't have kids, there are other options. And I know this is crazy and I'm not saying that we will end up together and have a family. But I want you to know if that's where we end up, I'm okay with it, with all of it."

My heart feels like it's going to beat out of its chest. I have this beautiful, amazing woman standing in front of me, telling me she wants to be with me in spite of me lacking the most basic part of being a man. I want to grab her and kiss her, to claim her as mine. I want to taste her again and feel content lying in bed with her at the end of the day. I want to feel loved for all of me, scars included. I slowly make my way towards her, reaching my hand out to touch her cheek. She closes her eyes and I wipe the tear that breaks away.

"Peyton," I whisper. "You're...incredible. I cannot believe you would be willing to do that for me."

I'm seconds away from accepting her offer and yet I can't. It would be selfish of me to let her live her life without being able to give her the gift of a real family. She would always know in the back of her mind that she had to give a dream up to be with me. I love her too much to ask her to do that.

"Of course, I would do that for you. I love you, James!"

Her words mean more to me than she can ever know. My heart breaks for what I have to do. I know I need to let her go, it's what is best for her.

"I love you too, Peyton. I need you to know that. I need you know that my life changed the day you walked into my office. I'll never be the same man. But...I can't let you give up that life for me."

I see her smile fall the instant she realizes what I just said, and I hate myself for it.

"What are you saying?"

"I'm saying that you are too amazing to settle for the life that I could give you. You deserve a man who can give you a real family, the kind that you grew up with. The kind that you have been dreaming of. I am not that man. I can't give those things to you and I will not be the one to take that away from you."

"James, I don't understand. I said that I am okay with not having those things."

"But I'm not with being the one to take them away from you. I'm sorry, I wish things were different."

The look on her face right now is filled with so much hurt and confusion that I almost second guess my decision. But I have to stand firm with what I'm doing, I know it's the right thing.

"You're serious right now?" her voice rises. I can tell she is turning from shock to anger.

"One day you will thank me." I try to continue but she cuts me off, throwing her hand up to stop me.

"Don't! Don't you dare say that! You're such a coward. I'm beginning to think you don't even *want* this. That it's all just an excuse to hide away from the world and live in fear and resentment."

She turns around and is out the door before I have a chance to respond. I feel the emotions brimming to the surface, begging to break free. I wipe away the single tear that I have failed to hold back and shove the rest back down, where they belong.

"I'm right. I *know* I'm right. She will see it someday," I try to tell myself.

I head over to my bar to pour myself straight up bourbon in an attempt to numb the pain. I think back to the words that Margaret had used on me. Telling me that I'll never be enough for another woman. These words anchor me, keeping me in check so that I don't run out the door and beg for Peyton to take me back.

I already know there will be no one else like her in my lifetime. She could handle all of me, my dominant side in the bedroom, my past, my flaws. There will never be another that will understand and accept me the way that she does. I just gave up my only chance at real happiness in this world. The reality of it is too much to bear sober. I ditch the glass and begin to drink straight from the bottle, passing out shortly after.

Chapter Twenty-Five

Peyton

I spend the remainder of the weekend hiding out in my apartment eating my bodyweight in cheesecake. I ordered an entire new york style cheesecake from my favorite bakery down the street and am ashamed to say that there is not much left. I watched movies from my childhood that always bring me back to a simpler time in my life. *Sixteen Candles*, *Dirty Dancing*, and *Father of the Bride* were on constant rewind in my teen years. Back when you had to sit there for what felt like an eternity while the VHS player rewound the tape. I felt marginally better by the end of the weekend.

After calling Blake and ringing her ass for not telling me she was pregnant, she made me tell her what had me so down. She was eventually able to somewhat convince me that James had his own problems to deal with and this had nothing to do with me. Although, there is still a voice inside my head telling me that I was just not good enough. That one day, the right woman will come along, and James will give her everything he can. If I'm still at his company when that happens, it will be a soul crushing day.

I'm stuck in my head when I step into the elevator and don't realize who is standing there until I'm already on, and the doors are closing. James is in his dark gray suit that always makes me feel weak in the knees when I see him in it. My treacherous heart would like to cry and plead with him to want me, but I thankfully have enough pride to hold it all in.

"Peyton," he begins to say.

"Just stop," I speak softly. "Please just give me some time before you...we...before we put this behind us and pretend it never happened. I just need you to leave me alone. We can talk during our meetings with the consultants if it's necessary. Other than that, I need you to give me space."

I don't dare turn my head to look at him. Keeping my head down is my only option to get out of this elevator without crying or hitting him. I hear him exhale like he wants to say something, but the rest of the way up is ridden in silence.

Later that evening, I'm spending the evening with Liam and Harper. My brother has taken this challenge and showed just how strong he is. He has such an amazing connection with Harper, it's precious to watch him interact with her.

"You've been doing such an amazing job with her, I'm so proud of you," I tell him as I lay next to Harper on the floor as she plays on her mat.

"She makes it easy. She eats and sleeps well," he says while taking a sip of his beer on the couch.

"Quit being so stubborn and give yourself some credit."

He chuckles at my frustration. "Okay, fine. Thank you for your kind words, sis."

"That's better. Isn't it, sweet girl? Is your daddy the best?" I babble to Harper.

"So ah, Mom told me about your troubles with your boss. How are you holding up?"

"Ugh, of course Mom did, and his name is James."

Why is everyone so intent on bringing him up? I should have kept him away from my family. Now I'm paying the consequences of that choice.

"Sounds like he had a pretty rough childhood. Don't take it personally sis. These are his issues that he needs to work through. You're an amazing woman who is going to find a man that will fight like hell to keep you. If James is not that man, that is his loss."

"I can't stand that, *it's his loss*. No offense but if that's supposed to help me feel better, it's not working."

"I know, that was a total cliché thing to say, but... it doesn't make it any less true." He looks at me earnestly.

"Thanks."

The doorbell rings and interrupts our little moment, though I cannot say I'm sad about the disruption. Liam puts his beer down on the coffee table and heads towards the foyer while I continue to play with Harper on the floor. She's kicking her arms and legs as they hit the toys hanging from her mat. I'm so thankful to have this little peanut in my life right now. She's a ray of sunshine no matter what is happening around me.

When Liam walks back into the room, he's accompanied by someone I recognize as Becca's friend although I cannot recall her name. She is carrying bags of diapers and wipes as Liam holds a bottle of wine.

"Peyton, this is Becca's friend Riley. She has been helping out with Harper."

Riley waves at me as she walks over to the changing table and begins restocking everything. She clearly seems very comfortable in my brother's home right now. I can't help but feel a little tense as I watch her in action. Liam comes back with a glass of wine and hands it to her.

"Come sit down and join us," he tells her.

I watch them sit down and start chattering about Harper and her feeding and sleeping schedule. They keep trying to bring me into the conversation, but I'm too stuck in my head to make any good conversation. I conclude that I'm overreacting, and Riley must just want to make sure Harper is being taken care of. Either way, I decide to give them space and tell them I need to get back to the city. As I drive back, I try to reason with myself that my brother would not move on from Becca so soon, and with her best friend. However, my gut is telling me that I am correct in my assumptions.

I'm going to table this for now, until I am in a better mental place and can think it through. The last thing Liam needs is for me to accuse him of something that is possibly all in my head. At least tonight was successful in one thing, distracting me from my broken heart.

Chapter Twenty-Six

James

I'm on my way to Ralph and Melinda's house right now even though it is not Monday. I was in no shape yesterday to see anyone after my horrible encounter with Peyton in the elevator. It tore me apart to hear her ask me to leave her alone. I was prepared to skip this month's visit, but Melinda was not having it.

"Hello, dear." Melinda squeezes me as I walk into the house.

I walk into the familiar house where I spent almost half of my childhood and am surprised by the sense of calm I feel. Sometimes I forget that this place turned into my sanctuary when I was younger. The feeling of security still emanates from these walls.

"Ralph, James is here," Melinda shouts as we walk into the backroom.

"Nice to see you, son." He gets out of his chair and shakes my hand. "We missed you yesterday."

"Sorry about that, rough day."

Melinda ushers us into the kitchen as usual where the smell of her cooking wafts through the room. I sit down and take my usual seat, knowing if I tried to help Melinda would shoo me away. Ralph grabs two beers out of the fridge, placing one in front of me before he takes a seat.

"If it's been one of those weeks already, you can use one of these."

"Thanks," I say as I take the beer and enjoy a nice long swig.

"So, what's got you down this week? You never miss a Monday dinner," Melinda asks as she serves us and takes a seat.

"Oh, it's nothing to worry about." I take a bite of the meatloaf in hopes that we can move onto another topic.

"How is work?" Ralph asks.

"Not so fast," Melinda interrupts. "Now, I have let a lot of matters go that you do not wish to discuss. But I know you and I know that something is going on. You're going to fess up and tell us why you couldn't make it yesterday."

"It was just a woman I was seeing. We...ended things and I guess it has hit me a bit harder than I expected."

"Well, she must have been someone pretty spectacular to get *you* all worked up," Ralph says.

"Yeah," I shrug my shoulders. "She's amazing, but we had to end it."

"And why is that?" Melinda raises her eyebrows at me.

"Because I'm no good for her."

"Now that is the most preposterous thing I have heard in a long time. Why on earth would you think that?" Melinda says as she puts down her fork.

"Just trust me, okay? I know that I can't give her everything she deserves."

"Well, you're kind, handsome, and wealthy. What am I missing here? What can't you give her?" Ralph asks.

"I can't give her a child, okay?" I slam down my fists on the dinner table.

They both look at me still and wide-eyed. I see Melinda's eyes become misty and wish I could get out of this conversation. The pity I'm going to receive is more than I can bear right now.

"What are you talking about?" Melinda speaks up.

"Margaret and I found out during our engagement that the night my old foster parent beat me, he didn't just leave a bunch of bumps and bruises, he took away my ability to have children."

Melinda reaches to her right to grab my hand. I look up at her and see the pain in her face.

"Sweetheart, I'm so sorry. Why didn't you tell us?"

I shake my head. "I didn't want anyone's pity. What could anyone do about it anyways? I'm broken and can't give any woman what they want most in this world."

"Where on earth did you get that idea? There is so much more to you than just your ability to conceive. Is it Margaret? Did that horrible woman say something to you?"

It's incredible how Melinda was able to guess that right away.

I shrug my shoulders. "She said I was damaged and could not offer her or any woman what they deserve."

"Now you listen to me," Melinda slams her hand on the table. I look up at her and can feel the anger radiating off of her. "Margaret was a selfish woman. She was only looking out for *herself*, and I'm not the least bit surprised that was her reaction to your situation but what she said is not true. There are plenty of men *and* women out there who can't conceive for many reasons and *none* of them are broken or damaged. It just means they may have to look at alternative ways to have a family."

"Is this why you and this new woman aren't together? Did she tell you she couldn't be with you?" Ralph asks.

I sigh. "No, she told me she loves me despite of it and wants to be with me." I can see Melinda's eyes light up, but I continue. "But I told her she deserves someone who can give her a *real* family."

I see Melinda and Ralph exchange a knowing look.

"James, what is a real family to you? Ever since we took you in, you have kept us at arm's length. We have done everything we can to protect you and give you the love you deserve, but you would only let us get so close. Even today, you only come to see us once a month on a schedule, like we are part of your business. We have told you countless times that we want to see you more, but you refuse. We even wanted to adopt you when you were younger but were too afraid to even broach the subject with you. I know you had a rough life. You were dealt a hand that no child should be dealt, but you can't keep everyone at arm's length to protect yourself. It's not only hurting others who want to get closer to you, but it's also hurting you."

"I know bu...," I try to say but Melinda cuts me off.

"I'm not finished," she takes a deep breath. "I'm sorry for everything that you have been through. But please don't push away this girl out of fear. You say you can't give her a *real* family, but what you have failed to see is that family looks different in many homes. We're a family, the three of us. Why do you think Ralph and I have no children?" she looks at me with a questioning eye. "It's because we couldn't conceive ourselves."

I sit there listening to this woman admit to me that she couldn't have a child of her own, and I feel an enormous amount of guilt wash over me. They decided to take in a foster child to become a family, and all I did was keep my distance.

"We're a family, whether you acknowledge it or not. We are a family because we love each other. You could have a family; you could give someone a family. You can adopt or get a donor. What is going to make you guys a family is the love you share for each other and the memories you make with each other. So, I'm asking you to please think about it before you let this woman slip away."

I stare at her in total shock at her words. I had no idea they wanted to adopt me, that they cared about me that much. I have always looked at myself as an inconvenience to them, someone they pitied. All these years, I have been hurting them by keeping them at a distance. I don't know what comes over me, but I stand up and walk over to Melinda. I bend down and wrap my arms around her; the first real hug I feel I have had since my parents were around. One where I'm not protecting myself but accepting love. I feel the tears begin to well up and slide down my cheeks as I accept this woman's love for me that I have denied all these years.

We stay locked in each other's arms for several minutes as we both grieve for our losses. Our loss of being given the chance to feel what it's like to bring your own child into this world, and for the loss of all these years of words left unsaid. When we finally break apart, I stand up and see tears brimming over Ralph's eyes. This man is tough as nails. In all the years, I have never seen him shed a tear.

We compose ourselves enough to finish dinner and I make Melinda go rest as Ralph and I take care of the dishes. I'm rinsing as he loads the dishwasher.

"You know son, Melinda is right. If this woman."

"Peyton, her name is Peyton."

"Peyton. If Peyton loves you and wants to be with you, you can't let her pass you by. I can see it in your eyes when we bring her up or when you talk about her. You love her."

I nod my head up and down. I do love her. I love everything about her, and I was such a fool to turn her away. I know I don't deserve her forgiveness, but damnit, I have to try.

Chapter Twenty-Seven

James

At work the following day, I'm a nervous wreck as I try to decide the right time to talk to Peyton. I know most woman want a well thought out romantic gesture, but I can't find it in me to hold this in any longer. I ordered hundreds of roses to be delivered to her office this afternoon, begging the florist for this morning but she couldn't get them delivered that soon. Now, I have to wait half the day and pretend like I have the capability to get a single thing done until then.

I spent most of the night trying to come up with these big, elaborate ways to get her to forgive me. All of the ideas took time to plan and execute. Truth be told, I don't know what the hell I am doing. I know the talk with Melinda and Ralph yesterday opened my eyes to a lot, but it can't erase my past and the trauma. I'm still fearful that one day Peyton could wake up and decide she didn't realize what she was committing to and leave me. However, I don't want to be the reason for anyone's unhappiness anymore, including my own.

It's just after lunch time when I get a notice that the flowers have just been delivered. With that, I check myself in the mirror before I take the elevator down to her floor. I see the commotion of people walking by her office in shock as they peak in, offering a jab or a laugh before they head back to their desk. When I reach her door, I see her standing in the middle of the room gazing at the roses that take up most of her office. Wow, I didn't realize how overwhelming roses could smell when there are so many of them in a small space. I shake my head at how much I am already messing this up.

She must sense someone behind her because she quickly turns around until we are face to face. I see tears glistening her eyes and have to resist the urge to take her in my arms.

"What's all this?" she whispers as she gestures to the room.

I sigh, looking at the clutter of roses. "It's one rose for every time I'm likely to mess up or let you down in the future."

"What are you talking about?"

"Peyton, I'm so sorry for pushing you away. I was scared and weak. It had nothing to do with my feelings for you. In fact, I feel so much for you that I was afraid of getting hurt." I take a deep breath and push continue. "Gosh. So much of my life was spent getting hurt that I was afraid to open up to anyone. To give anyone the power to leave another scar. I have realized that it's not only hurting the people around me but it's also hurting me, and I don't want to do that anymore. I know the way we have started this is not traditional or romantic, and I know having to think about kids before we have even been on a proper date is backwards, but I love you. I want what we had and so much more. If down the road we decide we want a family, I want it with you in whatever way you are comfortable with. You're so amazing and generous to come to me and offer those things and I will spend forever trying to earn your forgiveness for turning you away. Please, tell me you still want this."

Somewhere during my speech, I ended up only a foot away from her. She has a steady stream of tears running down her cheeks, and I reluctantly reach out to wipe them away with my thumb.

"I'm so sorry," I whisper.

"James," she looks down, shaking her head. My heart is beating out of my chest waiting for her reply. When she looks back up, she is biting her lip as a small smile begins to form. "I love you!"

She wraps her arms around my neck, and I take her in my arms and hold onto her. When we finally release each other, I wipe the remaining tear from her cheek and softly press my lips to hers. It's a slow and tender kiss but it does not lack in intensity.

"Oh gosh, I almost forgot we're in the office," she pulls away, running her hands through her hair.

I take her back into my arms, not ready to let her go yet.

"Hey, you're mine now. It's about time everybody else knows, starting with your mother."

She throws her head back laughing.

"Oh gosh, you have some serious sucking up to do to her."

I shrug my shoulders. "I'm up for the challenge. Maybe we can take some of these roses to her after work."

She looks around her office. "These are beautiful, but what were you thinking?"

"I was thinking I screwed up and you can never have too many roses."

She smiles and kisses me on the cheek.

"That's very sweet, but you're helping me get these out of here tonight. The smell will only get worse as they die."

"Deal. Let's start by grabbing some now and taking them back to your place." I reach for a couple vases before she grabs my arm to stop me.

"Wait a minute, it's not even two o'clock yet."

I lean down and whisper into her ear. "I'm the boss and I haven't been inside you in way too long. So, grab what you can and get moving before I take you right here in front of everybody."

Her cheeks flush as she chews the inside of her cheek, contemplating whether or not she's going to listen. It takes her about ten second to grab two vases and her purse as she rushes for the elevators. I follow her, chuckling at how easy that was.

Once we get back to her place, we put the vases on the kitchen island. Before she turns around, I grab her ponytail and bend her over the island, leaning over her to whisper in her ear.

"I'm going to take you right here." She pushes her behind into my groan and wiggles it. I groan and smack her ass. "Fuck, I've missed this."

She turns around and starts unbuckling my belt. I work on the buttons on her blouse. In seconds we are both naked and grabbing at each other, not able to slow down. I lift her onto the island, grabbing her legs and wrapping them around me. Once I finally push into her, my entire body feels at home.

"Baby, I'm going to spend the rest of my life trying to be enough for you."

She grabs my face. "You've been enough from the very beginning. You will always be enough."

Epilogue

Peyton

4 Years Later

"I know what you said, but I need the timeline moved up. We have a big acquisition coming up and I need this project complete before we take that on. Thank you." I put the phone down and fall back in my seat. It's been one of those days. Luckily, James picked Mia up from daycare, so I have time to pick up dinner on my way home.

I look down at my growing belly and smile, thinking about what it will feel like to finally hold him in my arms. We just found out we were expecting a boy and James is on cloud nine. I'm not going to say the beginning together was easy. There were a lot of ups and downs as we navigated through James' past and his healing. Eventually, we found our groove and got married three years ago. James wanted to get started on a family immediately, and I was pregnant from a donor within three months. Mia is now a healthy eighteen-month-old. James took to fatherhood right away. That girl has her daddy wrapped around her finger.

When I walk through our front door, I hear laughter and giggles in the back room. I follow the familiar route to the toy room and find Mia giggling as she piles all of her stuffed animals on top of her daddy. Once she is finished, he jumps out of the pile and screams, grabbing her and bringing her down with him. I stand there smiling for a minute as I rub my belly, as Mia squeals with delight. I clear my throat to get their attention.

"Dinner's ready," I say as their heads turn in my direction.

"Mama!" Mia crawls out of her pile towards me. I crouch down and wrap her in my arms.

"Hi, baby!" I squeeze her. "Uh, I missed you!"

"Hi, mommy!" James shouts from the pile. "Come join us!"

"Daddy, it's dinner time."

James pops up and crawls towards me. "Get mommy!" he shouts to Mia.

They both jump at me and drag me down into their stuff animal oasis.

Mia giggles. "Mama!"

I can't help but laugh as these two throw animals around. I never would've imagined this future with James the first time I met him, but I'm so happy this is where life took us. I can't imagine a better partner in life. He has been the best husband and father.

"Alright you two, let's go eat dinner before it gets cold."

James grabs Mia and throws her over his shoulder as we make our way to the kitchen.

"How was work, babe?" James asks.

"Ugh, it was fine. Just getting pushback on my deadline, nothing I can't handle."

"I know you've got it babe. That's why you're my VP of IT." He winks at me.

Once Lance retired, I was made the vice president of IT. I told James I didn't want him making the decision, I wanted it left in the hands of Lance. He promised me to conduct a fair interview process. I still think Lance was bias, but it beat my boyfriend giving me the position.

After dinner, I give Mia a bath and read her a bedtime story. Once she is asleep, I kiss her forehead and tip toe out the door. James is relaxing on the couch when I get back to the family room. His face lights up when he sees me, and he pats the spot next to him.

"Come join me, babe," he says. When I sit down, he wraps his arm around me and places his other hand on my belly. "How are you two doing?"

"Oh, we're just perfect. He's starting to get a little rowdy in there, but I'm loving it."

"Have I told you lately how much I love you?" he asks.

"You tell me every day, babe," I chuckle.

"Well, that's still not enough," he says before he kisses me. "Oh, I forgot to tell you that Melinda and Ralph want us to come over for dinner this weekend to celebrate the news of a baby boy."

"Of course," I say. James' relationship with his foster parents has grown so much since we first got together.

I'm so proud at how much he opened up to them and allowed them to love him. It didn't come naturally to him at first, but he kept trying.

I rest my head on his shoulder. After a couple minutes, he begins to slowly rub his hand up and down my thigh. I squirm every time his hand goes up, hoping he will keep going higher, but he never does. I take him by surprise when I straddle him and begin to move left to right on top of him.

"What is this about?" he asks in surprise.

"Are you kidding me right now? You kept teasing me with your hand on my thigh."

His head falls back as he laughs. "I didn't even realize I was doing that. You have become such a horny little one lately, I'm liking it."

"Shut up and kiss me."

He continues to smile as I attack his mouth. Eventually, the kiss turns hot and he groans as I continue to work my hips back and forth. I can't believe this man ever thought that he couldn't give me everything I needed to be happy. He picks me up and carries me to the bedroom to remind me why he will always be enough.

About The Author

Nicole loves writing romance novels that feature a strong female lead who knows what she wants in and out of the sheets. She writes about real struggles and real people who are trying to find happiness in love and life. She lives in Cincinnati, OH with her husband and two daughters.

Books Also by
Nicole Baker

Nicole Baker

Printed in Great Britain
by Amazon